House of Durand 4

embrace of the vampires

ERIN BEDFORD

Also by Erin Bedford

The Underground Series
Chasing Rabbits
Chasing Cats
Chasing Princes
Chasing Shadows
Chasing Hearts
The Crimes of Alice

The Mary Wiles Chronicles
Marked by Hell
Bound by Hell
Deceived by Hell
Tempted by Hell

Starcrossed Dragons
Riding Lightning
Grinding Frost
Swallowing Fire
Pounding Earth

The Crimson Fold
Until Midnight
Until Dawn
Until Sunset
Until Twilight

Curse of the Fairy Tales
Rapunzel Untamed
Rapunzel Unveiled

Her Angels
Heaven's Embrace
Heaven's A Beach
Heaven's Most Wanted

House of Durand
Indebted to the Vampires
Wanted by the Vampires
Protected by the Vampires
Embrace of the Vampires

Academy of Witches
Witching On A Star
As You Witch
Witch You Were Here
Just Witch It
Summer Witchin'

Granting Her Wish
Vampire CEO
The Beast of the Fae Court

House of Durand 4

embrace of the vampires

ERIN BEDFORD

Chapter 1
Drake

I HELD MY GOBLET of wine in both hands as I slouched in my seat. Lord Bolton's wife threw her head back against the lounge chair and laughed, her breasts shoved out toward my twin and me. My head rolled to the side as I licked my lips. It hadn't taken much convincing to get an invitation back to Lady Jocelyn's rooms. In fact, it had only taken a few, well-placed compliments and a whispering of what my brother and I could do to her. Lady Jocelyn was more than...eager to let us demonstrate.

"Why, Allister, you sly dog." Lady Jocelyn slid her stocking-clad foot up the inside of his leg and stroked up and down his length.

"One would think you are asking me to betray my husband and master."

Allister cupped her foot in his hand. Leaning down to press his lips against her ankle, he slipped his hand up her calf and under her skirts. "What gave me away?"

Closing her eyes, she let out a low groan. "Ah, Allister, you do have a way with your hands." Her eyes slitted open, her hooded gaze shifting to me. "And what of you, Draconius? How are you with your hands?"

My lips ticked up at her question. Taking a final drink of my wine, I sat it on the table next to me before shifting out of my seat and down to the ground before her. Taking her hand in mine, I pressed my lips to each knuckle and turned her hand over to suck on the pulse on her wrist. It jumped at my kiss. Lifting my eyes to meet my brother's, but not removing my lips, I felt hunger pulsating within me. Not for sex. For what lay beneath Lady Jocelyn's skin.

Opening my mouth, my blunt teeth lengthened and scraped against her skin. Lady Jocelyn jumped with a slight yip, but allowed me to hold on to her wrist—until my fangs sank into her flesh. Her scream of pain barely registered as the hot liquid filled my mouth, and I gulped down the delicious life force, unable to get enough.

Allister opened his jaw wide, his own set of fangs flashing at Lady Jocelyn, causing her to fight us even more. It was useless, of course. We were too strong for the lady used to fine things and simpering fools. My mind filled with nothing but the taste of her blood and the need for more.

When her cries of terror and pain ebbed, and her blood slowed, I lifted my head and startled. Dropping the wrist in my hand, I jolted back from the blank, dead eyes of not Lady Jocelyn, but Piper Billings.

I came awake with a jerk, sitting up in bed so fast that the world spun, my skin damp and my pulse racing. My eyes whipped from side to side as I searched for the remnants of my memory turned nightmare. Thankfully, the body of our maid and newly made human servant was nowhere to be found in the basement where my brothers and I slept during the day.

Scrubbing a hand over my face, I threw my legs over the edge of my bed and sat there, breathing deeply. I looked over the other five beds and thankfully found them empty. I didn't know if I could handle questions from my brothers right now. Especially not from Rayne. The mind reading, nosy busybody.

Sighing, I stood and stretched, letting the muscles in my body lengthen, pulling the stiffness out of them. Scratching my chest, I headed to the bathroom to relieve myself and shower. I'd have to ask Darren to clean my sheets. We still didn't let Piper down here, even though she was Antoine's human servant.

Turning on the hot water, I dropped my shorts and stepped under the spray. My mind raced with what my dream could have meant. It wasn't unusual for me to dream of my past. I remembered Lady Jocelyn well, however, the events didn't go quite like my dream.

Allister and I weren't vampires when we bedded the fair Lady Jocelyn. We'd been humans. It had been the last day we'd been human actually. Her husband had come home shortly after we'd bedded her, and we'd had to sneak out the window to get away. That was how the master had found us. He turned us and made us use our abilities to get into any woman's bed to get ahead in anything he needed—politics, wars, business. Whatever he wanted, we did. Whether we liked it or not.

I shuddered, even beneath the heat of the water.

Seeing Piper's dead eyes staring back at me was something I never wanted to witness. While I was still getting to know the maid, I didn't want anything bad to happen to her. Specifically by my hand.

Banging on the door pulled me from my thoughts.

"Are you going to stay in there all day or what?" Allister asked from the other side of the bathroom door. "We kind of have a situation."

Growling at the lack of privacy in this house, I turned the shower off and grabbed a towel. Drying off, I wrapped the towel around my waist and jerked open the door. Allister stepped back so I could pass. "What is it?"

Allister looked me over, far more observant than I would have liked. "You look like hell."

I snorted. "Thanks."

Allister's eyes burned into my back as I moved to my dresser and pulled out a pair of jeans and a tank top. I could already feel the need to pound something with my fists building inside of me.

"Are you going to tell me what's going on, or are you going to stare me to death?" I rolled my eyes over to him as I tugged on my shoes.

Crossing his arms over his chest, Allister narrowed his eyes on me. "If it would work, I'd gladly do it. What happened?"

Letting out an exasperated sigh, I tied my shoes with a rough jerk. "Nothing, just a bad dream."

"A bad dream?"

I nodded, swallowing thickly. "Remember Lady Jocelyn?"

Allister's face paled. "Of course. What about her?"

"Well, let's just say our past came back to haunt me, but ended with us killing Piper." I stared off to the side, unable to bear seeing the expression I knew was on his face.

Allister closed the distance between us, his hands clamping down on my shoulders, and he shook me slightly. "It was just a dream. You didn't kill Piper. We didn't kill Piper. She's upstairs right now, driving the whole household crazy with her cleaning madness."

My gaze jerked to his, the matching set of swirling blue eyes met mine. "Cleaning madness?"

Dropping his arms, Allister sighed, his lips tugging down at the corners. "Yeah, seems Wynn's sacrifice has affected her the most."

I scowled. "Sacrifice? Is that what we're calling it?"

Allister narrowed his eyes on me, aggravation making him frown harder. "Yes. He sacrificed himself to save Piper."

"It isn't a sacrifice, it's suicide," I argued, pushing past him to the stairwell. "You know what the master will do to him, make him do." My stomach rolled just at the thought. Giving up Wynn was the stupidest thing we ever did. Even if it did save Piper.

Allister's footsteps were hot on my heels all the way up the stairs. Pushing the door open, he jerked me to a stop with his hand on my shoulder. "What?"

"Wynn will be okay. We will get him back."

There was such conviction and certainty in his voice, I wanted to believe him, but it was hard. Instead, I nodded curtly and left him at the stairs to enter the dining room, where I found Darren setting the table and Rayne watching Piper on a step ladder.

"How long has she been doing that?" I pointed toward Piper, who was expending way too much energy on cleaning the drapes of the dining room at six o'clock at night.

Darren made a distraught sound and continued to set the table. "Since before dawn. She came beating on my door looking for her list of chores before I'd even gotten out of bed."

I sighed and crossed my arms. "That can't be good for her."

"Better than her bawling her eyes out in bed." Rayne gestured toward her with a frown on his lips. "I had to sit with her until she passed out from all the crying."

"Fuck," I cursed and shook my head. "We need to get Wynn back. Now."

We watched as Piper climbed down from her ladder and scurried over to us, covered from head to foot in dust. With a bright smile that I wished was real and not forced, she told us, "All done with the drapes. Let me just shower and then I'll get started on the windows in the library."

"Actually," Darren interrupted her, grabbing her by the elbow. "I need some help in the kitchen. Gretchen is out for the evening and I cannot read her gibberish handwriting."

Piper's brows furrowed, not quite believing Darren. It was complete BS. Darren and Gretchen had been working together for years. If anyone could decipher her handwriting, it'd be him, but I didn't call him out on his fib and neither did Piper.

"Okay," she drawled, and let him lead her away.

"How likely do you think it is she'll figure out what Darren is doing and our food ends up burnt?" I slid my gaze from where she disappeared over to Rayne.

Lips twisted into a grimace, Rayne shook his head. "Better practice your face now, because who knows what will set her off again."

Fuck.

Rubbing a hand down my face, I glared at the floor. Ever since Wynn was taken, all of us have been a bit on edge. Especially Piper. She took it the hardest. She didn't understand why we would just let Wynn take her place. I didn't really understand it either, but I knew we couldn't let her die for it.

Sadly, it wasn't the first time one of us had to hand ourselves over to the master to protect someone else. All of us had our turn with the master. I shuddered, remembering my time under our master's thumb. It was nothing compared to Rayne's time. Unless we could finally kill the bastard, it wouldn't be the last.

My eyes went to our younger brother. His mop of auburn hair seemed more unkempt than usual. I didn't envy his place as comforter, though I could take up the job of consoling in a different manner. Crying women were not something I was good at.

Though, for Piper, I might be able to figure it out.

I'd always been attracted to the human maid, but now that she was officially a permanent fixture in our family, I wanted to know the tantalizing female more intimately. Leaning over so I could see into the kitchen and get a glimpse of Piper's backside through the open door, I smirked. Very intimately.

"Hey." Rayne smacked me on the arm with a scowl.

"What?" I rubbed my arm where he hit me and held back a smile. "I can look, can't I?"

Rayne crossed his arms over his t-shirt covered chest and leveled me with a glare. "You don't have ogling rights until you spend hours wiping her tears away and telling her it's all going to be okay."

My lips quirked up at the edges, and I patted Rayne on the shoulder. "You've got that part covered, little brother. I'll just leave the comforting to you and enjoy the fruits of your labor."

Shoving my hand off his shoulder, Rayne prodded a finger into my chest. "You haven't earned the right to even leech off of my good boyfriend points. Do I need to remind you about your comment at the ball? She just works for us?"

I groaned at the admonition of my stupidity, lifting my eyes to the ceiling. Sometimes, I didn't know why I even spoke. Dropping my gaze back to Rayne, I arched a brow. "Boyfriend, huh? Have you asked Piper about this new label you've put on yourself?"

Rayne's face hardened. "That's between Piper and I. You can just butt out."

I lifted my hands in defense. "Hey, you don't have to bite my head off. I just wanted to know if I should be expecting wedding bells soon."

Rolling his eyes, Rayne shook his head, his eyes drifting toward the kitchen door. "I don't see how that would even work. Not that it's on my mind." He shot me a look before continuing, "She's Antoine's human servant, plus there's Wynn. I don't think marrying me would even work with all the other players in the mix."

I lifted a shoulder and dropped it. "You never know." I stepped toward the hallway, intent on going to work off some steam, but then stopped and turned back. "Does it bother you?"

"What?"

"Sharing her?"

Rayne placed his hands on his hips and shook his head, a small smile on his face as he chuckled. "I'm surprised you even have to ask. You share with Allister all the time. Does that bother you?"

I snorted, crossing my arms over my chest. "No. We share everything."

Instead of answering, Rayne held his hands out in front of him as if to say, see?

Nodding in understanding, I headed out of the dining room and down the hall. So many thoughts swirled through my mind and there was little I could do to fix them. All I wanted to do was hit something. Hard.

Chapter 2
Piper

RAYNE'S AND DRAKE'S EYES followed me into the kitchen. While Darren headed to the fridge, I sat down at the island, tapping my nails in an impatient rhythm on the granite countertop.

I wasn't stupid. I knew they were trying to distract me. Right now, I was happy for it. I needed it. Because if I stopped, even for a second, I would think of Wynn and what he gave up for me. My eyes still burned from my crying session last night. Thankfully, Rayne had been there beside me the whole time. I didn't know what I would do without him. He held me all night, even when I was bawling like a baby—and I mean *really* crying. We're talking snot, drool, tears, the whole nine yards. Not something I wanted to repeat. So, keeping busy it was. I hoped that by the end of the day, I'd be so tired I'd pass out without thinking of Wynn or...Valentine.

Most nights I was fine, my mind too tired to dream, but other nights... Those nights brought back everything that happened at Boris's manor, and to my utter horror, repeats of what Valentine did...had almost done to me.

I could still feel his hand gripping my face, keeping me from calling out to the others. Could feel his fangs in my throat as he drained the life from my body. I rubbed the side of my neck, even though there weren't any visible scars. All my scars were inside, quivering like the scared little girl I was turning into.

"Are you alright, Piper?" Darren turned from the fridge, his arms full of ingredients he would need for dinner. Unlike the rest of us, Darren seemed as put together as ever. His ebony hair was slicked back against the top of his head. His suit, as impeccable as always, clung to his form, his white gloves spotless. While they would have looked strange on someone else, I'd grown used to him, and they were just part of who he was.

"Why do you wear those gloves?" I inquired, instead of replying to his question.

The answer wasn't something I wanted to talk about.

Arching a brow, Darren placed the items in his arms on the counter between us.

My eyes skimmed the ingredients—milk, celery, tomatoes, red and green peppers, cheese, and eggs. What was he making?

"When I first began to work for the Durands, I didn't wear them," Darren explained, as he organized the items on the counter. He turned and pulled a bowl down from the cabinet next to the stove. "As you've learned, sometimes our job entails cleaning up blood. Other people's blood, their blood. And it can be..." He trailed off, looking for the right word.

"Messy?" I supplied, placing my elbow on the island and leaning my face on my palm.

Darren smiled slightly and nodded. "Yes. I found more often than not I would end the day washing blood from my hands." He held his hands out, staring down at them as if there was blood on them now. There wasn't. The gloves were as white as newly fallen snow. With a slight shake of his head, Darren went back to work, pulling out a knife and a cutting board. "It is much easier to bleach the gloves than to try and get the blood off my hands and out from under my nails." The last bit was said with a sort of forlornness.

My heart ached for him, and I had the sudden urge to hug him. So I did. Standing up from my seat, I rounded the counter with Darren's watchful eyes on me. I took the knife from his hand. He let me and turned my way. Stepping closer, I slid my arms around his waist and hugged him. Not just for him, but for me.

For a moment, I wasn't sure if he would hug me back, but then slowly, Darren wrapped his arms around my shoulders and held me tight. We stood like that for a few minutes before I moved out of his embrace, a small smile on my lips.

"What was that for?" Darren asked, picking the knife up once more and placing the celery on the cutting board.

I shrugged. "I wanted to. You seemed like you needed a hug and maybe..." I sighed and glanced off to the side, my voice going low. "Maybe I just needed one."

Darren inclined his head as the crunch crunch of the celery being cut filled the kitchen. I handed him the next stalk when he was done, swiping the sliced pieces into the bowl. We worked in silence for a few minutes. Once we finished the celery and tomatoes, we worked on the bell peppers next.

My nose scrunched up at the smell and I made a face.

"Don't like peppers?" Darren chuckled and smirked.

Holding a pepper out like it was a snake about to bite me, I shook my head. "No way. Peppers of any kind really. They just taste blech."

Laughing at my expression, Darren worked on shredding the cheese into the bowl. When that was done, he poured milk in and then cracked the eggs. He whipped them all together before moving to the cabinet on the other side of the stove.

Returning with a bag of flour, he motioned toward the bowl. "Will you stir?" Nodding, I took the bowl and spoon from him. He didn't even measure as he poured it in a little bit at a time while I mixed.

"How do you know how much to put in?" I cocked my head to the side, watching as the concoction thickened and turned into more than just a glob of ingredients.

"I've been doing this for a long time. Measuring doesn't make sense when I know what it should look like after each ingredient is added. Besides, my grandmother never measured and taught me the same way." Darren's lips ticked up in a genuine smile.

I'd never heard him talk about his family. I only knew he had grown sick and Antoine had saved him. None of the others talked much about their pasts. Not unless I asked directly. With all that had happened, their pasts were the last thing on my mind.

Sighing at my lack of culinary genius, I finally gave in and questioned, "What are we making anyway?"

Throwing in a handful of spices, Darren went to the fridge and grabbed a silver container, which I knew contained blood. "Blood bread pudding." The expression on my face must have been horrible, because Darren added with a twinkle in his eyes, "It's not for us. Not unless you've gained a taste for blood?"

I shook my head rapidly. "Nope. I'm still fully human..." I paused and tapped my chin in thought. "I guess I am. Except for the whole human servant thing. Besides not aging or getting sick, and Antoine being able to feel my emotions, what else should I expect?"

Darren poured the thick red liquid into the bowl, and I held back the urge to vomit. Nope. Not into blood. Not one bit.

"You shouldn't expect much else. You already know about the heightened senses and the attraction." He gave me a sideways glance at that, making my cheeks burn. "It wouldn't be unheard of to be more attracted to those who are also blood bonded to Master Durand."

I rolled my eyes. "All these years and you still call him Master Durand," I mocked, huffing my chest and holding my arms in front of me like a puffed-up gorilla.

Darren's lips twitched. "Habit."

My eyes followed Darren's movements as he poured the mixture into a pan before turning to the oven. He'd preheated it without me knowing, allowing him to slide the pan right inside. Intent on keeping the conversation on him and my mind off what I really wanted to obsess about, I leaned back against the counter. "Can I ask you a question?"

Darren set the timer and then began working on the dishes, unable to stand still for one moment. "You will anyway, so go ahead."

Chewing on my lower lip, I angled my head to the side, trying to watch his expression. "You and Antoine..." I started, my cheeks burning at what I was about to ask. "You're lovers, right?" His face didn't change, which made me nervous and word vomit. "I mean, the others kind of already implied you and him, you know, bump uglies, but you don't really act like a couple and, well..." I trailed off, realizing that if they were lovers, then Antoine had practically cheated on him with me.

"Yes, I suppose you could call us that, but please do not feel guilty on my account," Darren said over his shoulder, his hands busy with the washing. He'd replaced his white gloves with plastic ones, and it looked so ridiculous with him in his suit that my lips twitched.

Pushing my smile down, I shoved away from the counter and placed myself at his elbow, leaning so I could see his face. "I mean, I'm already boning Rayne and Wynn, it's not like I don't see that you guys all like to share. So, I guess it's not really a big deal, but I can't help but wonder...do you love him?" I paused for a breath, and then clarified, "Antoine, I mean."

Without stopping what he was doing, Darren hummed, rolling my question over in his mind. "Love is not big enough of a word for what I feel for Master Durand." I made an annoyed sound. "Antoine."

Happy that I was making baby steps toward breaking him of the habit, I rested my face on my fists as I bent over the counter. "So, what's it like then? Love is kind of the ultimate emotion, isn't it?"

Darren's hands stopped for a moment, his eyes glancing up to the ceiling as he thought. "In this day and age, love is something you throw around so easily, it is hard to tell who actually means the words and who is only saying them just because. However, what I feel for Antoine is far greater than love."

I angled closer to him, intrigued by his explanation.

"I respect him," Darren continued, returning to his washing. "He gave me a chance at a new life. Something I hadn't even been given the option of by my own family, who threw me away the moment I got sick." Rinsing the dishes, he handed them my way. I picked up the towel on the counter and began to dry them, my attention focused more on him than getting the dish dry. "Master—" I cleared my throat. "Antoine, listens to me, heeds my counsel, and yes we are lovers." He ended with a confident, "I belong to him."

I frowned at the unfinished statement. "But shouldn't that mean he belongs to you too?"

Darren smiled, a genuine one that didn't hold any sadness or bitterness. "He cannot belong to me and be what he needs to be for everyone else."

His words gripped my heart and I had the urge to hug him again.

Seeming to realize what I wanted to do, Darren held his dish glove covered hands up and shook his head. "Do not pity me, Piper. I don't. I am happy with my life. I have more than I could have imagined for the station I had been born into, and in a world where love and marriage were a contract between families for wealth and power, Antoine has given me far more than I ever hoped for."

I opened my mouth to argue the fact, but Darren stiffened, his eyes whipping to something behind me. As I turned, Antoine's voice filled the kitchen.

"I am glad to hear you feel that way, Darren." I thought for a moment he was mad or even making fun of Darren's confession, but when I was able to lay my eyes on Antoine, I saw it was the truth. A softness I hadn't seen before covered his face and his lips curled slightly at the edges as he watched the butler next to me.

My gaze bounced between Darren and Antoine, trying to figure out how the dynamic between them worked, but I was at a loss. I didn't think I could live with someone, be their lover after all these years, and not expect love in return. However, the way the two of them looked at each other with such utter devotion and care, maybe they knew something I didn't.

Darren was the one to break the silence, inclining his head slightly. "Dinner should be ready in about twenty minutes."

"Excellent." Antoine finally allowed his gaze to drift over to me. "I hope you can learn from Darren's example if you are to stay my human servant, Miss Billings."

My eyes narrowed on Antoine, my jaw tightening. "So, it's Miss Billings now?" Crossing my arms over my chest, I glowered at the finely dressed vampire. So put together. Not a single strand of silvery blond hair out of place. His blue eyes locked on me with a curious expression. The emotions I'd been holding back spewed out of me without warning. "You can bite me, fuck me, make me one of you, but you can't call me by my first name. It's no wonder you let Wynn be taken. We're all just employees to you. Who will be next? Huh?" I shouted, moving forward until I was at the island, my hands curling around the edge of the counter. "Rayne? The twins? Or maybe Darren? I don't know how anyone here can stand to look at your face let alone love you."

Antoine didn't yell at me like I expected and perhaps wanted. Instead, his expression went neutral, his words low and restrained. "If there is something you wish to complain about, *Piper*. Please do not hesitate to let me know. I am, after all, a fair employer."

"Employer," I spat out, the fire in me building to epic proportions. "That's all I am to the lot of you, aren't I? Some pathetic employee who let her hormones get the best of her, while you all think screwing someone is just another day in your long, immortal lives. You sexist, fascist pig!"

"Piper—" Darren touched my arm, but I jerked away from him.

"You might be happy being his butt boy, but I'm done." I shoved away from Darren, throwing my hands out in front of me. "I quit!"

Seething at the whole thing, I stomped around the island and up the stairs. I didn't stop until I reached my room, where I slammed the door shut, locking it. My eyes scanned over the area, searching for my bag. I found it under the bed and threw it down on top. I went to my dresser and began pulling armloads of clothing out and tossing it into the bag. Opening my drawer, I grabbed the books and other things inside it, putting them into the bag as well. A clink in the drawer drew my attention.

An empty vial.

The same vial Wynn had used to heal me when Rayne had accidentally broken my hand. It had rolled out from where it had been hiding and sat there gleaming in the light. Beckoning me to pick it up.

My fingers slowly reached out and grasped it. The rage in my chest exploded into sobs as I clutched the vial to my chest. Sinking down to the ground, I cried into my hands, my knees pulled up to my chest as I rocked.

I was such a fool.

Chapter 3
Antoine

DARREN WATCHED PIPER STORM away with his mouth agape. I sighed and shook my head. I could hardly say I was surprised by her behavior. From what Rayne had reported, Piper was torn up about Wynn's capture. It only made sense she would blame me for it. I blamed me.

"Antoine—" Darren stepped toward me, but seemed to catch himself. "I mean, master." He bowed at the waist, making me sigh once more.

"Please stop that, Darren." I used two fingers to urge him up. "Piper is right. We've been together far too long for you to keep calling me that in private."

Darren nodded, lifting his head. After a moment, he glanced toward the staircase once more. "Perhaps I should go speak with her? I don't know what came over her. She was fine a few moments ago."

I waved him off. "No, leave her be. She needs time to cool off. Besides, she's not wrong."

"Piper doesn't understand. She's upset." Darren tried to make excuses for her, but they weren't needed. I knew exactly how she felt. "It's not your fault Wynn was taken."

"Wasn't it?" I countered sharply. "If I had taken care of Boris before this, we wouldn't have even been in that situation. We wouldn't be constantly looking over our shoulders if not for me. I'm supposed to be the master of this household and I couldn't even keep one of my own safe."

I released a heavy breath, my face going into my hand as anguish consumed me. Darren touched my arm, and I lowered my hand. Removing his glove, he lifted his palm to my face. I leaned into his touch, needing it at that moment more than anything.

"You have done more for this household than any of us could have ever asked for. You cannot place the burden of everything on yourself. Were there things that could have been done differently? Of course, but there are seven other people, not counting Piper, that are more than willing to help you with your load. Let us help you. Don't put the blame all on yourself."

"Six," I corrected, placing my hand on top of his before removing it from my face. "There's six. Wynn is gone. He can't help us now."

Darren's lips curved up. "Do you really think he isn't trying to right now?"

My lips twitched. "I suppose you're right."

Nodding, Darren turned back to the stove. "Now, go sit down. I'll bring you some wine and the food will be done soon."

I sniffed the air. "Is that your famous blood bread pudding?"

Giving me a sly look, Darren picked up an oven mitten and waved it in my direction. "Perhaps. I suppose you'll just have to wait and find out."

My stomach grumbled with anticipation as I headed for the door. Pausing with my hand on the frame, I turned back to Darren. "I am, you know."

Darren busied himself with the wine, not looking at me. "You are what?"

"Yours." Darren's head snapped up, his dark eyes meeting mine. "As much as I am able to be."

Stunned by my words, Darren stared at me for a long moment. Then seeming to remember himself, he straightened and jerked his head up and down twice before turning back to the wine.

Heading into the dining room, I tried not to let what Piper said bother me too much. God knew I was already kicking myself enough for what happened. Not only to Wynn, but to Piper. Something I hadn't said to Darren was how much I actually knew about how Piper felt. Valentine's attack on her bothered her far more than she let on. Her dreams were evidence enough, even if I couldn't feel the despair inside eating away at her. So, if I had to be the bearer of the rage, then I would do so proudly.

Allister already sat at the table with Marcus. Draconius was nowhere to be seen, but the faint sound of pounding against sand in my ears told me he was in the gym. This wasn't the first time the vampire used his fists to beat away his problems. I could probably go for a few rounds myself. If I had the time. As it was, business came second and making sure my family was safe came first. My own feelings would have to wait.

"What was all the commotion?" Allister asked with raised brows, his fingers twirling an empty wine glass on the table. "It sounded like a banshee howling in the moonlight."

I shook my head, taking my seat. "Don't worry yourself. There are more pressing matters."

Rayne glared at me hard. No doubt knowing exactly what had happened in the kitchen. Yet he said nothing. Instead, he shoved his chair back and left the room without a word. I pushed a thought to him. *Please make sure she's alright.*

Stopping in his tracks, Rayne turned back, surveying me and my thoughts for a moment before the anger on his face dissipated. With a curt nod, he continued toward Piper's room. If anyone was going to be able to calm her, it would be him.

Marcus appeared in the doorway a few moments later. His towering height made him look menacing and it had served me well in the past as well as the present. I counted on him to have my back and provide me with the much needed show of strength I required to keep my house from being attacked by other vampire masters.

I sat up straight in my chair and turned my gaze on him. "Well?"

Taking his seat next to me, Marcus placed his fists on the table. "There's no word on where the master has gone. No trace of his entourage either."

"How is that possible?" Allister scowled, throwing a hand up. "There's at least a hundred of them living there in that ghoulish manor. "How could no one know where they went?"

"There's more," Marcus proclaimed, just as Darren came out of the kitchen. He walked around the table, pouring wine into our glasses. He lingered next to my chair, holding my glass out to me. My gaze met his as I took it, making sure our fingers brushed. Pleasure permeated from him at the gesture before he walked back into the kitchen.

Turning my attention back to Marcus, I lifted my glass to my mouth. "Do go on."

Lips pursed tightly, Marcus held his own glass in both hands. "Morpheus claims he knows something about their whereabouts."

My back stiffened at the name of the vampire master playing club owner in Savannah. Morpheus dallied in vampire politics far too well and I didn't trust a word that came from his mouth. Unfortunately, we didn't have the luxury of ignoring his claim.

"What did he have to say?" I inquired, sipping my wine.

Darren came out of the kitchen once more, his hands covered with the oven mittens, and he waved at me while he carried the glass pan. Blood bread pudding wafted through the air and all three of us inhaled with appreciation.

As Darren filled our plates, Marcus returned to the question I'd asked. "He wouldn't say over the phone. He will only tell you if you come to his club. Claims you have neglected him for far too long."

A snort from the doorway pulled my gaze that way. "He always was a pretentious bastard." Draconius entered the room, freshly showered. He ran a hand through the short top of his hair and took his seat. Picking up a fork, he scooped up a large portion of his blood bread pudding and shoveled it into his mouth. "You should send him one of his human servants' heads in a basket."

I grimaced at the food rolling around in his mouth. "Still, he has all the cards and we, unfortunately, don't have any. We can't return his offer of information with an act of violence. No matter how well deserved." I settled a look on Draconius before cutting into my own meal.

Allister chuckled. "Morpheus has more human servants than vampires. It's not like he would miss one."

Draconius laughed with his twin.

I found myself smiling despite myself. My eyes scanned over the table and landed on Wynn's empty chair. The laughter drained from my face. No, as much as I wanted to show the pretentious bastard, as Draconius had described him, a lesson, we couldn't risk Wynn's safety. Any information would be more than what we had now.

Returning my attention to Marcus, I leaned back in my chair and pointed my fork lazily in his direction, hiding how affected I was by Wynn's loss. "There's no sign of our master at any of his other estates?"

Marcus shook his head once, taking a bite of his food.

I hummed. "Well, I suppose we should provide Morpheus with exactly what he wishes." Sitting up straight in my seat, I skimmed my eyes over my brothers. "Make the arrangements for Savannah." I stopped for a moment and then looked to the twins. "Someone will need to stay with Piper."

Draconius was the first to protest. "And miss out on Club Dead? No way. I haven't gotten a chance to go down there in years." Memories of Morpheus's club, Club Dead, filled his eyes, and I couldn't blame him. There were so few vampire clubs anymore and Morpheus's club, whether I liked it or not, was one of the best in the country.

"Very well," I drawled out, turning my gaze to his twin. "I can assume you will want to accompany your brother."

Allister had the good sense to at least seem contrite. "If that's alright with you. Who knows what this idiot will get himself into without me there." He nudged his brother with his elbow right when he was taking a drink.

Draconius choked on his wine and banged on his chest, trying to dislodge the liquid. While we didn't particularly need to breathe, we needed air to speak. When Draconius could talk again, he turned a glare on his twin. "I don't need a babysitter."

Allister snorted. "Sure, you don't."

The other twin opened his mouth to argue more, but I cut them off. "Then I suppose we'll have to—"

"I'll do it." Rayne appeared at the doorway, his arms crossed over his chest. There was a tiredness to his voice even though his gaze hardened. "I'll watch over her. Someone has to. Might as well be the one person here she trusts."

No one argued with him. Sadly, it was true. Right now, Rayne was the only one—perhaps besides Darren—who Piper trusted. She still blamed me for Wynn's capture. The twins had put their foots in their mouths far too many times, and Marcus...well, who knew with him. Though, he had made his opinion known on the female human turned human servant far too many times for her not to have noticed his disapproval.

Picking up my wine glass once more, I nodded in his direction. "Very well. It's settled. We'll leave tomorrow. Be ready."

Rayne took his seat at the table and Darren came out to fill his plate and wine glass. We didn't need human food, but there was no way we were bringing in someone from the donor service tonight or any night until we knew our master wasn't planning on attacking the rest of us. Traveling to Savannah was going to be a big enough risk without inviting snakes into our home.

"Darren." Draconius caught my human servant's attention, patting his stomach. "That was delicious. I don't know why you don't make it more often."

One who didn't know the butler would have said he didn't react to Draconius's compliment, but I could tell he was preening inside. Not only because I could feel it, but because his eyes lit up and his chest puffed out slightly.

In response to Draconius's question, Darren replied, "If we had it all the time then you wouldn't appreciate it when I did make it."

"Yes, I would," Draconius argued, but Darren was right. We often took for granted something that was always there. Once more, my eyes drifted to Wynn's empty chair next to Rayne's.

Twirling my wine glass between my fingers, I pushed some power behind my words. "Leave Darren alone, Draconius. You're dismissed."

The loud-mouthed twin got to his feet, affected by my powers, but seemed to have enough will to grab his plate and head for the kitchen. Probably to stuff his face more. Allister followed his brother with an apologetic smile to Darren. Marcus finished his meal in silence before he, too, left—most likely to check on our transportation to Savannah—leaving only Rayne, Darren, and myself.

I didn't dismiss Darren, allowing him to linger while I turned to Rayne. "How is she?"

Rayne sighed, cutting his blood bread pudding into tinier pieces than necessary. "Tired, distraught, beating herself up for blowing up on you two."

I hummed and nodded. "That's expected."

Picking up a piece of food, but not putting it into his mouth, Rayne turned to me. "Why didn't you set her straight when she yelled at you?"

I dropped my gaze from his, staring into my wine glass. "Because she was clearly upset. I can't hold her human emotions against her. The change is too new. She will feel everything tenfold." I shifted my eyes to Darren. "If I struck down all my human servants for being emotional, then I wouldn't have any." A tiny smile crept up my face at Darren's flush.

Rayne, oblivious to the double entendre in my words, huffed and put his fork into his mouth. "Still, I'd have liked to see her call you, what was it again? A sexist, fascist pig?" His mouth quirked up at the edges, laughing at my expense.

I harrumphed. "Not the worst thing I've been called."

Chapter 4

Rayne

AFTER DINNER, I HEADED back to Piper's room. I didn't trust her being alone. I wouldn't want to be alone right now.

Wynn may have been a lot of things—rake, manwhore, a big pain in the ass—but he was the heart of this house. The one who taught us not to run headlong into danger when we could be doing other more pleasurable things. He made us stop and think in his own twisted, sex crazed way.

I missed him.

Feared for him.

I knew what it was like to be at the mercy of our master, and while I had gotten the worst of it, Wynn was next in line. Having the ability to seduce anyone might sound like an awesome power, but when used by Boris? It could make even the most pleasurable activity into one's worst nightmare.

I thought we were done having our powers used against us. I thought we were finally safe. Now it's started again. Though, this time, I wasn't so sure we'd get out of it sane, if at all.

Rapping my knuckles softly on the door, I listened for Piper's voice. Soft breathing answered me. Confident she was sleeping, I twisted the handle and inched my way inside.

Piper lay spread out on her bed. Her blonde hair splayed around her head like a halo, her mouth slightly ajar, making me smile. Closing the door quietly behind me, I walked the length of the room, removing my shoes before I slid into the bed next to her. My lips twitched as she curled toward me, wrapping her arm around my waist and throwing a leg over my own. I stroked her hair and gazed down at her.

I didn't know how lucky I could be. Life had been a series of unwanted thoughts and rash decisions just to feel something new. Then she came into our lives, this annoyingly perky human with a penchant for getting into trouble herself. And she wanted me.

Me. The youngest of the Durand house. Without an active power. Sure, reading minds was useful for planning an attack or knowing your enemy's secrets, but it didn't help when it came to a real battle. I'd felt pretty useless for the longest time. Now, because of Piper, I didn't.

This. I brushed my fingers along the side of her cheek, and she moaned and leaned into my touch. *This was what I was made for.*

"Rayne," she murmured in her sleep, her hips rotating against my side.

I arched a brow. *What was my girl dreaming about?* Leaning down, I pressed my forehead against hers, closing my eyes as I concentrated. I pushed my mind into hers, searching for what had Piper so worked up.

Inside Piper's head, she and dream me were in the bathroom, soaking in a bubble bath. Interesting that she would choose the bathroom for her fantasy. I'd have to remember that for later.

In the tub, Piper sat in front of me with my arms wrapped around her. However, one of my hands had dipped down to cup her breast, tweaking her nipple between my fingers. Piper's head fell back onto my shoulder, where dream me dipped his head down to brush my fangs against her neck.

My interest rose as Piper moaned even louder, rubbing herself against my dream self. I could feel my physical body hardening in response to the sounds she was making. Tired of being on the side lines, I pushed myself further into her dream, replacing dream me with my own consciousness.

The taste of Piper's blood touched my lips as my fangs sank farther into her neck, savoring the taste of her on my tongue. The water swished against my sides, warm to the touch. Piper's slick form pressed between my legs. Her backside rubbed and arched against my cock. I thrust my hips into her ass, my hands gripping her tighter to my front. My fingers slid down her body, brushing against her breasts, skating across her stomach, before dipping between her thighs.

Piper gasped, her hands coming up to tangle her fingers into my hair. "Rayne, please."

I stroked my finger along the length of her folds, circling around her clit before pressing a digit into her center. Her hips jerked into my hand as I pumped it in and out of her. In real life, Piper wouldn't let me do this. She was too torn up by what happened to Wynn. She hadn't let me so much as kiss her, but obviously, from what she was dreaming, she wanted it. At least on a subconscious level.

Releasing my fangs from her neck, I licked along the bite before pressing my lips against her ear. "What are you so afraid of?"

Piper jumped in my arms. Her head whipped around to face me. Her eyes widened as she realized it wasn't just her dream anymore.

"R...Rayne?" Her words ended in a gasp and groan as I added another finger inside of her. "W-What are you d-doing in my head?"

I smiled against her temple. "Well, you're wrapped around my body, rubbing yourself against me like a cat in heat. I had to see what was in that pretty little head of yours." I cupped her breast with my other hand, squeezing it tight, causing her to arch into my hand. "It seems you've been holding back." I flicked her clit, making her thrash in my arms. "So, tell me, Piper, what are you so afraid of? Why are you holding back?"

Piper moaned and rode my hand, not answering my question.

I stopped, pulling my hand away.

"No, nooo, don't stop," Piper cried out, grabbing for me. "I need...I need..."

"Is it Wynn?" I probed, not giving her what she wanted. "Do you think because he's gone you can't be happy?"

Piper turned her head away, her face pressing into my arm. "No. I mean, yes. I guess." She sighed and sank farther into the water. "I guess I do feel a little guilty. Because I'm safe. I have you and the others." Her voice grew low and quiet. "He has no one."

My heart sank to my stomach. Wrapping my arms around her, I held her tightly to my chest. "We will get Wynn back. I promise. We already have a lead."

"You do?" She jerked upright and the world around us shimmered. She was fighting to wake up.

Sending an apology to my hard-on, I withdrew from her mind.

Lifting my head from hers, I blinked my eyes open.

Piper's light brown gaze narrowed on me. She pushed away from my chest and sat straight up. "Spill."

Annoyed at myself for letting the tip from Morpheus slip, I rubbed a hand down my face. "Antoine's going to kill me."

"You're already dead." Piper poked my chest, her teeth gritted. "So, tell me already."

Sighing, I sat up as well. "The master vampire of Savannah has a lead on where Wynn could be."

"Okay, then let's go." Piper moved to get out of the bed, but I grabbed her arm.

"Hold up there, sparky." I pushed her back down with a shake of my head. "Morpheus isn't someone to be trifled with. He owns a club that caters exclusively to vampires. He has demanded Antoine come in person to get the information."

"Okay? And that's a problem why?" Piper cocked her head to the side, frowning. "It's just a vampire club. I lived through your master's house of horrors, couldn't be worse than that."

I chuckled darkly. "Oh, it can. Morpheus is...tricky. He might say he wants to help, but that help always comes with strings." I brushed her hair behind her ear and cupped her face in my hands. "We can't give him anything he can use against us."

She sank into the bed, her bottom lip pushing out into a pout. "Meaning me."

"Exactly." I leaned in and kissed her, nipping at her lower lip. "I couldn't handle it if anything happened to you."

Nodding, Piper pressed into my arms, letting me embrace her. "What are we going to do then?"

Holding her close, I kissed the top of her head and stroked my hand up and down her hair. "Exactly this. We wait and let my brothers take care of Morpheus. We can't put you in any more danger than we already have."

I tried to peek into her mind, but the moment I touched it, her hand slipped beneath my shirt, her nails scratching against my stomach. I lifted my head, peering down at her. A coy expression filled her eyes as she looked up at me beneath hooded eyelids. Her hand shifted downward until her fingertips snuck beneath the waist of my jeans. When she brushed against the top of my cock, still hard from the dream, I sucked in a breath.

"Piper," I questioned, not wanting to make her stop, but not sure if she really wanted to or if it was just because of what I said. "We don't have to—"

Her hand wrapped around my full length and gave me a firm tug. "Does it look like I want to stop?"

Gulping, I licked my lips and shook my head. "No, but I just don't want you to—"

"Rayne," Piper interrupted me once more, pumping her hand faster as she slid over into my lap. "Shut up and kiss me."

Not one to look a gift horse in the mouth, I pulled her more firmly against me, my hands settling on her ass. Her pajama shorts rode up, and I took full advantage, slipping

45

my hands beneath the fabric to palm her flesh.

Piper groaned and pressed back into my grasp, her hands busy unsnapping my pants, freeing my length from the tight constraints of my jeans. Shifting so I was laying completely on my back, I watched her rock her hips in rhythm with her hand. As much as I loved watching her and feeling her touch me, I wanted more. Needed more.

I grabbed the top of her shorts, and with a rip of fabric, split them down the middle. Piper gasped and narrowed her gaze on me.

"I liked those shorts."

I smirked, smoothing my hands over her bare flesh. "Well, I like them better on the floor in pieces." Piper snorted, releasing my cock to cross her arms, gripping the bottom of her shirt and pulling it over her head. Her breasts sprang free and I leaned up to latch my mouth around one nipple, using a free hand to palm the other one.

Arching into me, Piper gasped and shoved her heat closer to my erection, her wetness causing her to slide up and down my length. Releasing her nipple with an audible pop, I placed both hands on her hips and moved her faster against me. While I wanted to be buried deep inside her, the small sounds she was making, the mews of pleasure and gasps of delight, were too good to stop.

Her nails bit into my shoulders, her eyes fluttering shut as she threw her head back. Piper's body rocked with her orgasm and my eyes flickered to the pulse in her neck. My fangs ached and begged to be buried inside her, but I wasn't sure if she would be alright with it. Sure, in a dream was one thing, but in real life? That was a whole other thing entirely.

"Do it," Piper breathed.

My gaze jerked up to meet her now open eyes, her head angling to the side as she pushed her hair off her shoulder. I licked my lips, my fangs pressing against the back of my mouth. "Are you sure?"

Piper's face hardened, and the next thing I knew her hand was between us. It was my turn to gasp and moan as her sweet muscles tightened around my cock. She rode me at a rough pace that had my head spinning, and if I needed to breathe, would have had me catching my breath.

While I was distracted by the movements of our lower halves, Piper's fingers tangled into the back of my auburn hair and gripped it tightly. She angled her neck more and pushed me toward the pulsating vein just beneath the surface. "Do it, Rayne. Please."

It was the please that got me.

Baring my fangs, I latched onto her neck, piercing her flesh with my teeth. When her delectable blood filled my mouth, I almost orgasmed on the spot. I pushed it back, reminding myself I had more self-control than that. Wrapping one arm up and around her shoulder, and the other around her waist, I bore down harder on her neck, thrusting my hips up to meet her body.

We moved in tandem, the slick sound of our bodies colliding against one another as we each chased our release. Somewhere in my blood and sex filled mind, I knew this was a distraction. Either for her or for me. It didn't matter either way, all I wanted was Piper and for once, for this one moment I had her, I never planned to let her go.

Chapter 5
Piper

I WAITED UNTIL I was sure Rayne was asleep before I slipped from the bed. I stared down at the redheaded vampire and smirked. Human or vampire, they were all the same. Get them off and they slept like the dead. Literally, in Rayne's case.

Shaking my head as I smiled, I moved over to my dresser and slowly opened the drawer, aware of any and all sounds that might wake my keeper up. I grabbed a pair of sweats and pulled them on, then reached for an oversized shirt, pulling that over my head next. Forgoing shoes, I inched toward the bedroom door and eased it open. A slight creak made me wince. I paused, glancing back at the bed where Rayne grunted and turned over but didn't wake.

Letting out a slow breath, I slipped out of the bedroom door and closed it quietly behind me. Out in the hallway, I leaned over and breathed heavily, my heart pounding like a jackhammer in my chest.

It was hard working for and dating vampires. It was especially hard to lie to one who could read your mind. I might have told Rayne I would leave it alone. That I would let them take care of it and stay behind, but it wasn't in my nature. There was no way I was going to let them do this without me. It was my fault Wynn was taken. It only made sense for me to be the one who helped get him back.

I padded down the hallway, my feet barely making any sound on the carpeted floor. I passed Darren's room, which was as quiet as a mouse. He was probably already asleep. It was past three a.m. and the only ones who would be awake at this time were vampires. Except for Rayne. I smirked to myself again.

Passing the staircase, I leaned over the edge of the rail, angling my head to the side as I strained to listen for the others. One of the benefits of being a human servant was the heightened senses. Sucked balls for my emotions, though, which was evident by my freak out in the kitchen earlier. I just hoped I'd be able to put a lid on those sooner rather than later. Darren seemed to do fine. I didn't think I'd ever heard him raise his voice like I had. It made me hopeful for more control in the future.

Voices reached my ears, but they were muffled, too far away for me to figure out what they were saying or who they were. They were most likely in the basement. At least the twins were.

I glanced away from the stairs toward the opposite side of the hall from my room. One person wouldn't be down there. The one person I wanted to talk to, and I knew exactly where he would be.

Antoine.

If anyone was a workaholic, it was him. He'd be up and in his office until well past dawn. Even then he took his work downstairs with him sometimes. Not that they had let me down in their little sanctuary yet. Bitterness filled my heart.

While some of what I had said to Antoine hadn't been true. Other parts, the employee part, still stung a bit. Three of them have had sex with me and yet, I was still denied being more than just an employee. I didn't know my place anymore. Were we still only employee and employers? Was I more? Did being a human servant mean anything?

Based on how Darren acted, it didn't seem like it. Though, the way he talked about Antoine...I stopped walking toward the office and sighed. I didn't know what was going on inside me or the others.

Gathering my courage, I moved toward the office door. I didn't knock, the doorknob was unlocked. I didn't know a time when it had ever been locked before. I guess when you were a vampire, you didn't care if someone interrupted you. You could hear them before they came in. However, with all that knowledge, I couldn't understand the sight before me.

The moment I stepped into the office, my mouth dropped, and my feet froze in place. My eyes focused on the silvery-haired vampire, his head thrown back and his eyes closed. His hand was on the back of Darren's head as it moved up and down in his lap.

I guess Darren wasn't asleep after all.

At my gasp, Antoine's eyelids lifted open, his head lazily turned toward me, his hand tightening in Darren's hair, urging him to keep going. Darren didn't stop what he was doing. It obviously didn't bother him that I was in the room while he sucked Antoine's dick. I honestly didn't think it bothered me. Not in a bad way.

Licking my lips, I felt heat pool between my legs where Rayne had been earlier. I pressed my thighs together, shifting in place as I watched them.

Antoine's pale blue eyes locked on to mine, the sight before me so erotic that I couldn't look away. His other hand lifted from the desk and gestured me forward. I found my feet moving of their own accord until I was at the edge of his desk.

I could see Darren more clearly now, his mouth moving up and down Antoine's shaft. Need pulsated through me and I curled my fingers into a fist to keep myself from going around the desk and taking Darren's place.

Out of all the vampires I worked for, Antoine had always intrigued me. Attractive in that cold, statistician way. However, once I became his human servant, every part of me wanted to please him, to find ways to make him feel good—aside from my little outburst in the kitchen when my anger overcame my need to serve in that moment.

Now, though, every inch of me wanted to please him. My thoughts on going to the club weren't even registering in my mind anymore. I just wanted him.

Antoine, still holding my gaze, grunted, having reached his release. Loosening his grip on Darren's hair, he pulled a handkerchief from his pocket and handed it to Darren. The butler lifted his head, swiping the handkerchief over his mouth before standing.

Darren did nothing to hide the evident bulge in his pants, his eyes going to me, and he nodded before moving toward the door.

"Wait." Antoine stopped him with a lift of his hand. Turning those pale eyes back to me, Antoine angled his head to the side and inhaled deeply. Knowing what he could scent, my face burned. "I see you've finally calmed down."

I coughed and lifted my hand to my face, turning my gaze away. "Uh, yeah. Sorry about that."

Antoine held his hand up, stopping me from going on. "That's not what you came here for, is it?"

My eyes snapped back to his. "Uh, no. Though..." My gaze shifted to Darren and softened. "I am sorry for what I said. I didn't mean it. I know it's not your fault." My attention moved back to Antoine. "I was just so...angry."

"It's to be expected." Antoine inclined his head and then turned fully in his seat to face me. "Your apology, while appreciated, is not needed. You will feel a bit out of control for the first year or so—"

"A year!" I balked, unable to comprehend being so whacked for that long.

"It is different depending on the person, but it took Darren a year and he had far more control over his facilities than you do." Antoine gave me a pointed look that made me want to smack it right off his face.

"Fine, but I don't want to stay here while you do all the work finding Wynn. I can help." I placed both hands on the desk, leaning forward slightly. "I can't just sit by when I could be doing something."

Antoine didn't even try to argue. Almost like he knew I would come here to dispute it. "I figured Rayne wouldn't be able to keep this to himself. So, I have a proposition for you."

Pulling back from the table, I arched a brow. "What kind of proposition?"

A tinge of a smile flitted over his lips as he leaned back in his chair. "Going to Morpheus's club is dangerous. So much so that even a vampire is risking him or herself just for a taste of what Morpheus has to offer." He huffed a laugh. "Pain for pleasure. Sacrifice for salvation. That's Morpheus's M.O."

I glanced from him to Darren and shrugged. "And you're telling me this why?"

Antoine stood and stalked around the table, stopping next to Darren, his hand on his shoulder. "I want you to know what you are getting into."

"I know what I'm getting into—"

"No." Antoine cut me off. "You don't." His eyes trailed over Darren's face, his neck, down his chest, and lingered on the bulge in his pants. His hand reached out and cupped Darren in his palm. Darren made a startled noise but didn't stop Antoine from touching him in front of me.

"What are you...?" My mouth gaped, my body heating at the sight.

"If you want to go with us into the devil's lair, so to speak..." Antoine massaged Darren through his pants, his eyes on me the whole time. "I need you to prove to me you will do whatever is needed, no matter what." His head swiveled back around to look at Darren, his fangs peeked out as he licked his lips, obviously aroused by the whole situation.

I glanced from Darren to Antoine, trying to piece together exactly what it was he wanted me to do. When it dawned on me, I barked a laugh, causing Darren to startle slightly, but Antoine simply cocked his head in my direction. "You want me to fuck

Darren?" I focused my gaze on the butler. "No offense, Darren. Just...I didn't think you swung that way."

Darren's lips twitched, the first sign of a smile since I'd been in the room, but he stayed silent.

Antoine, though, had no problem voicing his thoughts. "So, it's only his orientation that stops you? Not the prospect of doing the act?"

Narrowing my eyes on Antoine, I crossed my arms over my chest, my hip popping out to the side as I surveyed him. What was his endgame? Surely, he was just trying to scare me into not going. Did he really want me to fuck Darren? In front of him?

"So? What is your decision?" Antoine inquired after a heartbeat passed.

"I don't know what the point of all this is." I finally sighed and dropped my arms. "What does having sex with Darren prove?"

"What will you do when we get to Morpheus's club? When he finds you to be a pretty little thing that he wants to sink his fangs into?" His tone implied that Morpheus might want to sink something else entirely into me. "Would you do it? To get the information we need to save Wynn?" Antoine released his hand on Darren's bulge, his fingers going to the zipper of Darren's slacks.

The sound of the teeth undoing filled the air between us. My eyes were drawn to Antoine's hand as it moved. Before he could pull Darren out of his pants, I took a step forward.

"Stop this," I hissed, my eyes moving to Darren's face. "Are you even okay with this?"

Darren's gaze locked with mine as a small smile played on his lips. "It's the nature of being a human servant, Piper. After a few centuries, things like sex...don't quite mean the same as they did when we were human."

We. He said it like I was part of it. Which I supposed I was. I was a human servant now whether I liked it or not. That didn't mean sex didn't still mean something to me. It did. However...

Jerking my gaze back to Antoine, I took the few feet needed to close the distance between us. My eyes still locked on him, I replaced his hands with mine, slipping my fingers into the hole of Darren's slacks. Darren hissed at the contact as my first and second finger wrapped around his length. With one hand around his dick, I used the other to push down my sweats, my oversized shirt the only thing keeping me covered.

Shifting my attention from Antoine, I focused on Darren's hooded gaze. Licking my lips, I took a step back and then another,

Darren moving with me since my hand was on his most private part. We backed up until my hips bumped the desk, and with Darren's help, I settled myself on top of it.

Releasing him, I placed a hand on the side of his face, determined to make sure this wasn't cold and unfeeling, like how they were trying to make it seem. Darren was my friend. I could have sex with him for a chance to save Wynn. I'd fuck anyone if it meant saving Wynn from that monster, Boris, and his whore of a vampire bitch, Theresa.

My legs spread and I tugged Darren forward by the loop of his pants. His cock bumped against my center, still aching and sore from my time with Rayne. I pulled my lower lip into my mouth, my breathing coming faster at what was about to happen. Out of all the men in this house, Darren wasn't even on the list of ones I thought I'd end up having sex with next. At least, not like this.

Sure, I'd had fantasies of him and Antoine together, me watching or maybe even joining them. None of those fantasies included me having sex with Darren for the chance to help Wynn. Now that it was happening, I didn't let myself think about how wrong this was.

Focusing on this moment, I lifted my face to Darren, tracing his jaw with my fingertips until my thumb slid along his bottom lip. Darren opened his mouth, sucking the digit inside, and then playfully bit down on it.

"I never figured you for being playful in the bedroom." I grinned and pulled my finger away.

Darren smirked, his eyes dark with desire. "There's a lot you don't know about me."

I hummed, amused by his words. "Well, let's see if we can fix that." I shifted my hips forward, putting a hand between us as Darren braced himself on the desk beside me. I lined him up with my core, rubbing against the tip of him, making us both gasp.

As Darren pushed inside of me, my eyes shifted to Antoine, who stood off to the side, not having moved an inch from where he had been. I wrapped my legs around Darren, angling my hips up to meet his thrusts. Antoine's eyes never left us, his lips pressed into a thin line, his brows drawn down. I wasn't sure if he was upset or happy about what was happening. When Darren reached his hand between us, circling my clit, I realized I didn't really care.

My head fell back, and I moaned at the feeling of Darren moving inside me. Darren was a lot larger than the others. Something I tried not to think too much about. I didn't want to compare any of them, especially not while I had one of them inside me. It wasn't fair to them.

Darren's head fell down between us, his thrusts becoming more rapid. We were both close, so close.

"Stop."

Immediately, Darren stopped and pulled away, turning his back on me. I lifted my head, my jaw tightening as I glared at Antoine for his interruption. "What now? You wanted me to have sex with him, so I did. Did you think you were going to scare me off?"

Antoine didn't look at me, his eyes on Darren. "I'll come see you later."

Darren nodded and walked to the door, not even bothering to look back at me.

Rage roared through me as I shifted to get off the desk. Faster than I could blink, Antoine was there, taking Darren's place between my thighs. His hand gripped the back of my neck and he brought his lips down on mine. Frustration and need still pulsated through me, even as my anger grew. I kissed him back, my hands going to his hair, tightening in his locks until he grunted. One of his hands wrapped around my waist, pulling me closer to him. I felt the tip of him against my center seconds before Antoine pressed inside.

Pulling away from his mouth, I glared at him, my teeth bared in a snarl as I shoved my hips against him. "You're an asshole, you know that?" I gasped and grunted at the rapid and brutal pace we were setting. I didn't really know what was going on with me, but I would worry about it later.

"I know," Antoine agreed in a clipped tone, his hand pulling my leg higher onto his back.

"And sadistic." I cried out when he hit a new angle.

"Yes," he hissed, his fangs bared now.

As if my body had a mind of its own, my head shifted to the side, exposing my neck to him. When he bit into me, I moaned long and hard, shoving him into me deeper. "A real fucked up piece of work."

Antoine didn't answer this time, his mouth and cock too busy for him to supply a reply. My mind fogged with lust, keeping me from saying anything further. The sensation of him pumping inside of me and the pheromones coming from his fangs were sending my mind into sensory overload. All I knew was that I was reaching for something. Something more.

When my pleasure crested, I threw my head back, my nails digging into his shoulders and head as I screamed. Antoine answered with his own roar of pleasure. His fangs slid from my neck as his release filled me. Seconds later, before we could even get our heads back on straight, the door to the office burst open. Rayne stood in the doorway, his eyes searching the room for a threat.

When his worried eyes landed on Antoine and me, he relaxed, his mouth flattening into a thin line. "I thought you were hurt."

I pushed Antoine away and hopped off the desk, pulling the shirt down to cover my ass. "Not any more than usual."

Antoine grunted, tucked himself back into his pants, and then walked around his desk, sitting down like we had just finished a business meeting. Not like we'd just fucked like rabid animals after his other lover worked me up.

Walking toward Rayne, I stopped before him, his hands smoothing up and down my arms. The expression on his face said he didn't know exactly what had gone on in here, but he didn't particularly like it.

Not looking at Antoine, I turned my head in his direction. "I think I proved myself."

"We leave at six p.m. so be ready," was his only response.

I nodded and allowed Rayne to lead me out of the office. Before the door closed behind us, Antoine's voice drifted out of it.

"You forgot jealous. Extremely and unforgivably jealous."

Chapter 6
Wynn

THE CHATTERING OF THE party around me buzzed in my ears. In the south of France, our master, Boris, seemed to think he had to have an event every single night. I was exhausted from all of the socializing, not to mention the drain on my powers from using them on every single person with even the smallest bit of importance. I missed home. The quiet nights with my brothers, the taste of Gretchen's and Darren's cooking, and especially...Piper.

She was undoubtedly blaming herself for my sacrifice. I wished I was there to comfort her. To be there to tell her it wasn't her fault. I would do it again a thousand times over. All for her.

I sighed, leaning back on the chaise of white velvet and gold tassels, twirling my wine glass in my fingers by the stem as I scanned the room. The manor in France was quite a bit larger than the one back in Washington. Unfortunately, it was just as gaudy with high, elaborate glass chandeliers in every room. Oriental rugs lay across every floor, and marble statues depicting the most explicit actions possible. How no one found his style utterly tacky was beyond me.

"Don't look so dreary," Theresa cooed, slinking over to my side. Her dark hair curled around her shoulders and draped over her breasts. Breasts that were barely concealed by the crimson dress covering her body. A large V-shape had been cut out of the front of it, stopping just above her navel. The sides and back were bare, with only a tiny strap around her neck to keep the fabric in place. If I wasn't already head over heels for Piper, I'd have enjoyed the glimpses of her skin and may have even taken her up on her constant open invitation to bed her.

However...

I narrowed my eyes on Theresa and lifted my glass to her. "I agreed to be part of our master's house once more, but nowhere did I promise to enjoy it."

Theresa smiled and laughed haughtily. "Your loss." She skimmed her hands over her hips and gave me a suggestive smile. "You don't know what you're missing."

Letting out another exasperated sigh, I replied, "Yes. I do."

Huffing at my response, Theresa turned on her stiletto heels and sought out someone else to seduce. There were enough human and vampire men and women present that it wouldn't be hard for her to find someone to warm her bed tonight. I, unfortunately, would find no solace here. Not tonight. Not ever.

I wanted to reach out to my brothers, to someone, but I knew if I showed even an ounce of rebellion to our master then he would go after Piper again. I couldn't have that. So, I played the part he wanted me to play, but I wouldn't be happy about it. He couldn't make me.

I lounged against the chaise once more, leaning my head back on the side. I might have looked like I was posing for a picture, but really I was just trying to imagine myself somewhere else. Somewhere with Piper.

I could see it now. She would push through the crowd searching for me, dressed in something I'd picked out for her. Something lacy and short, showing off her lovely legs and amazing ass. She'd search until she found me, lounging here, ignoring everyone else but her. When her eyes locked on mine, Piper would gasp and run to me, her arms wrapping around my waist, and her face burrowing into my white poet shirt. She'd make a crack about what I was wearing, something about my pants being poured on like paint, I'd make a sexy joke, and she would blush and giggle. Then I'd—

"Why, look what we have here," a woman purred in French, her perfume overwhelming my senses.

Without opening my eyes, I turned my face away from her, responding to her question in French. "Not interested."

"Do not be that way, *mon cher*, we could have a lot of fun, you and I." The undeterred woman sat on the edge of the chaise, her thighs pressing against my long legs. A hand curled around my upper thigh, dangerously close to my groin. "I've heard so much about you, Monsieur Wynn."

Growling softly in my throat, I lowered my arms and opened my eyes, planning to give the woman a piece of my mind. To my displeasure, our master and host decided to grace us with his presence at that moment.

"Ah, Wynn, I see you have met Mademoiselle Kerry, she controls the majority of the banking industry for the southern portion of France." Boris's mouth was partially closed as he spoke, hiding his sharp teeth from anyone who might cry vampire. His hideous skin and large ears were explained away as a skin condition. Humans believed what was logical and didn't usually search further into it. Thankfully for him, we were in a century where his looks would be considered offensive to mention rather than back in the old days when they would have called him a demon and came for him with pitchforks and a priest.

I grunted in response to his explanation, planning on turning my back on her once more.

Boris's hand came down hard on my shoulder, his nails piercing my flesh through my shirt. I winced, but if Mademoiselle Kerry noticed, she didn't comment. Her eyes were on Boris's face. Seemed not everyone could pretend not to stare. I knew I had a hard time not thinking about how monstrous he looked.

To match his blackened heart.

"Wynn, why don't you show Kerry one of the suites upstairs." His grip tightened on my shoulder and I knew it was an order, not a question. He wanted me to seduce her for some reason. Probably to take control of the money coming in and out of the country. He was so easy to read.

Mademoiselle Kerry ripped her gaze away from Boris's grotesque appearance to smile coyly down at me. "I would love a tour of this magnificent manor. Please, *mon cher*. Would you show me?" She stood and held her hand out, her wedding ring winking in the light.

Disinterest filled my every muscle, but I placed my hand in hers and swung my legs over the chaise. Boris's hand slipped away and the skin he had broken through closed up within moments. I was sorry I couldn't say the same for my shirt.

"Come, this way.' I looped her hand over my arm and led her through the crowd. Theresa gave me a wicked grin, saluting me with her wine glass before turning back to the group of admirers currently slathering her with compliments.

Sucking back the urge to throw a temper tantrum, I ushered Kerry out of the ballroom and toward the stairs. She clutched my arm close, her cheek rubbing against my bicep. I rolled my eyes up to the heavens, praying Antoine was working on finding me a way out of this situation. I didn't know how much more of this I could handle.

"How long are you staying in Nice? I hope not too short of a time." Kerry's lower lip, which she had coated in a deep red color, poked out as she pouted. "I would love to spend more time with you, *mon cher.*"

My jaw tightened. "I do not know. For a little time more, I suppose."

Kerry squealed in delight, clutching my arm tighter.

I sighed and walked with her up the long staircase. I didn't bother telling her about the manor. She didn't really care. Kerry only wanted to spend the evening with me, or from her words, even longer. I didn't need the distraction.

I didn't take her to my room, I didn't need the stench of her perfume lingering in my one sanctuary in this place. I stopped before one of the guest rooms. Turning the knob, I pushed the door open, revealing one of the many similar bedrooms in the manor. Kerry gaped at the room like it was one of the best things she had ever seen. As a person of power, I doubted it was true.

The red silk covered four-poster bed was big enough to fit six people comfortably. I had no doubts our master intended for me to start an orgy or two while he had me at his mercy. I didn't plan on giving him anything he wanted, least of all making me do anything Piper wouldn't have wanted—including bedding the pretty banker.

"Oh, it is magnificent." Kerry sashayed over to the bed, sliding her hand along the top of it, a seductive smile on her lips. She glanced back at me from underneath her lashes and ran her tongue across her lips. "Don't you think, *mon cher*?"

I leaned against the doorframe, trying to figure out how to get out of this one. Boris wanted her on his side. I couldn't just leave her here to hide in my room. I needed her to leave happy and willing to do whatever Boris wanted without compromising myself.

"*Mon cher*?" Kerry frowned, turning from the bed to face me.

Pushing away from the door, I closed it behind us. "Lay on the bed." I pushed power into my voice, not going for subtle. The sooner she orgasmed, the better.

Kerry climbed onto the bed without argument, her dress sliding up her legs. Laying back on the bed, she held her arms out to her sides as if she expected me to climb up after her. What she didn't know was that I didn't plan to touch her at all.

Taking a few steps across the room, I kept my gaze on her face, not once dipping beneath her neck. "Touch yourself."

Kerry didn't know why she did it, but she did what I demanded all the same. I saw the confusion on her face, but I pushed more power into my voice, into the very room we were in. Her pulse quickened, her thighs pressed together as her arousal filled my senses. She was close already.

I scoffed. Humans.

"Please," Kerry moaned, her hands sliding over her breasts, cupping them in each palm before she couldn't handle it anymore and shoved her dress up, her hand delving between her legs. With how worked up she already was, it didn't take long for her to reach her completion, her body sagging in the bed as she passed out from her release.

I grabbed a blanket from a chair off to the side and draped it over her, giving her a small amount of decency before turning to the door. My work was done, and Boris couldn't complain. I was going back to my room.

Unfortunately, when I opened the door, Boris and Theresa were walking by in a hurry. Frowning at their quick departure, I reached out and caught Theresa's arm. "What's going on?"

Theresa glanced to Boris, who had stopped as well, and he nodded his consent. Theresa looked back to me, her face pinched with worry. "We just got word there are hunters in the area."

"Hunters?" I arched a brow. There haven't been vampire hunters near us in a long time. Most of us stayed so far under the radar that it was easy to avoid them. They usually took out the vampires who went on rampages and didn't care who they killed in the process. That they were here did not bode well.

"The sneaky bastards caught a whiff of us from somewhere." Boris scowled, his fangs gnashing against one another. "I thought we were being so careful."

I crossed my arms over my chest and snorted. "If you call this being careful then you have become sloppy over the years..." The burning rage in his eyes made me add, "Master, I just mean that you aren't exactly, inconspicuous." I gestured around the house and over the railing. "The large house, the lavish parties. So many powerful people being drawn to one area and then suddenly changing their mind on policies and procedures." Before I knew what was happening, I was up against the wall with Boris's clawed hand wrapped around my neck, squeezing it tight enough that I had a hard time speaking.

"Do you dare question me?" Boris's spittle hit my face as he snarled.

I grunted against his grip and forced out what I could. "I mean, look at you, master."

Theresa appeared at Boris's side, placing her hand on top of his as she tried to placate him. "He's right, master. We haven't been careful enough. Too many people have talked of your greatness. It was bound to draw attention."

Boris growled once more, but then with a push, he released me. "Very well." He adjusted his suit jacket, a disgusting color of mustard orange that clashed with his skin tone. "I hope all has gone well with Mademoiselle Kerry?"

I coughed and stroked my throat. "Yes. She's resting."

"Good." Boris clapped me on the shoulder and grinned, a ghoulish sight for sure. "I wouldn't want this to be a total waste of time. Now, Theresa, let's proceed with the move. We'll head to the Frankfurt manor in a few days. We just have to hold them off until then." Theresa bowed slightly before disappearing down the hall, leaving Boris and I alone. Boris kept one hand on my shoulder and leveled a stern look on me. "I expect you to be ready to leave in the next few hours. We have a plane to catch." He turned but then paused, spinning back to me with a finger to his lips. "And I wouldn't think about warning your family. Not unless you would like to trade places with your lovely Piper." His lips curled up into a vicious smile. "I would enjoy breaking her spirit."

Gritting my teeth together, I forced myself to bow my head, though it killed me inside to do it. "Of course not, master. I am, as always, at your service."

Chapter 7
Allister

"THIS IS GOING TO be great!" Drake exclaimed, shoving his clothes into his bag with a big smile on his face. "I haven't been to Club Dead since...since..." He glanced over at me.

I sighed, sitting down on the edge of his bed. "Since the twenties."

Drake's brows rose. "That long? Man, what have we been doing with our immortal lives?"

"Keeping out of trouble, that's what." I picked up the clothes he tossed toward the bed, folding them and placing them into his bag. "Morpheus isn't to be trusted. You know that, we all know that. Going to him with so little information isn't smart. It isn't safe."

"Which is why we are all going." Drake walked into the bathroom, calling out through the door, "You worry too much, we'll be fine. Then we'll get the information from Morpheus and save Wynn. Everything will be fine."

I groaned and leaned my head back as I stared up at the canopy. "Stop saying it'll be fine. Nothing is ever just fine. Plus, we're taking Piper. That makes this all the more dangerous. Morpheus isn't just going to give us the information for nothing. He's going to want something in return."

"Then we'll give it to him." Drake came out of the bathroom, his toiletry bag in his hands. "And Piper will be—"

"Don't say fine," I growled, glaring at him. "Piper gets herself into more problems just doing her daily chores. Putting her in a club full of vampires is asking for trouble."

Smirking, Drake patted me on the shoulder. "Then we better make sure she fits in enough not to draw attention."

I snorted. "Good luck with that."

"No, good luck to you."

Frowning, I pushed up off the bed. "What do you mean?"

Grinning like a fiend, Drake tucked his toiletry bag into his suitcase. "You have been assigned to make sure Piper looks the part of doting human servant. One that comes to vampire clubs all the time."

"What?"

Drake chuckled and zipped up his bag, singsonging, "Good luck."

Jaw tightening, I marched toward the door. This was ridiculous. Everyone was bound and determined to get us all killed. We went through all the trouble of saving Piper, even Wynn sacrificed himself for her, and here we were putting her in harm's way again.

I couldn't do it. I wouldn't do it.

"Allister!" Antoine's voice came out of his office as I passed by it.

Great. Just who I wanted to talk to.

Walking into his office, I didn't stop until I got to his desk, slamming my hands down on top of it. "I won't do it. Piper shouldn't come with us. It's too dangerous."

Antoine didn't even look up from the papers sitting in front of him when he answered, "Piper has proved herself willing to do what it takes to get the information we need." I opened my mouth to ask how she'd done that, but Antoine didn't give me the chance. "I will hear no more about it. Is that clear?" His eyes lifted, those ice-cold orbs locking onto mine. "Allister? Do we have an understanding?"

Gritting my teeth, I bit out, "Yes. I understand."

"Good." Antoine stood from his desk and stepped over to his bookshelf, pulling a tome down to examine something on the inside. "Now, I want you to make sure Piper is clothed for the occasion and instructed on how she should act when we arrive at the club. We can't have her running her mouth off to the wrong person and end up getting killed before we even have a chance to meet with Morpheus."

"All the more reason to leave her behind," I grumbled, crossing my arms over my chest as Antoine glared at me. Dropping my arms, I groaned my frustration. "Fine. I'll make sure she's ready."

"Thank you, Allister." Antoine snapped the book shut and replaced it on the shelf. "We'll be leaving shortly, so I suggest you get to work."

Knowing when I was being dismissed, I pivoted on my heel and walked out of the room. It took everything I had to keep myself from stomping out and slamming the door shut. I was acting like a child, I knew it, but it didn't stop me from thinking this was a bad idea. Something bad was going to happen, I could feel it.

My next stop was to find Piper. If I had to get her dressed and briefed, I had my work cut out for me and I didn't have a lot of time. First off, was finding something to wear. We didn't have time to go to the store. So, I'd have to hope Piper had something we could use in her wardrobe.

Marching through the hallway, I stopped at Piper's room, but I could scent that she wasn't in there. Turning my head to the side, I inhaled deeply. Kitchen. Piper was in the kitchen. Changing my course, I started down the stairs, the voices of others reaching my ears.

"I appreciate your concern, Piper, but I'm alright. Really and truly. Do not trouble yourself," Darren reassured Piper, his voice soothing and firm.

"But he just made you stop like that, that can't be good for your..." She trailed off, and as I came around the corner, I noticed her face was as red as the apple in her hand. Her eyes were pointed at Darren's crotch and I knew I was missing something important.

Darren's gaze shifted over to me before he slightly bowed in my direction. "Master Allister, how can I help you?"

Piper spun around to face me once she knew I was there. Her face became even redder than before if possible. "Uh, Allister, hey, how's it going? Want some apple?" She held out her half-eaten apple to me as if that could take my mind off what they were discussing.

Making a face, I shook my head. "Uh, no. Thanks. Is there something I'm missing?"

Her face paled, and she shook her head rapidly as she stuttered, "N-No. Nothing. Nothing of interest."

Darren cocked a brow but said nothing, not that I expected him to. For the most part, Darren was pretty tight-lipped about everyone's business, including his own. I had no doubt that whatever was going on between the two of them—and I wasn't stupid enough not to think there was—was something of interest. The fact that Piper looked two seconds away from upchucking her apple at any moment was telling.

Leaving them to their secrets, I glanced over the outfit Piper was wearing. Jeans that hugged her hips and ass and a V-neck t-shirt that accentuated her breasts. Overall it wasn't a bad look, but it wasn't the look we were going for. It said she was about to clean the drapes, not the human servant used to going to vampire bars and clubs. We needed something dangerous, kickass, and hot. Something in black or maroon. Something that said keep your distance or I'll beat you down.

"Is there something on my face?" Piper's eyes widened, her hand going to her cheek, swiping at some imaginary food.

My lips quirked up at the edges and I took a few steps closer to her. Leaning an elbow on the island, I gestured at her clothes. "Please tell me you have something suitable to go to the club in?"

Piper's eyes darted to her outfit, her lips pursed tightly. Seeing my point, she placed a hand on her hip and glowered at me. "Of course I do. Did you think I was going to show up in this?"

"Then why are you wearing it?" I cocked my head to the side.

Smacking her hand on top of the island, Piper let out an exasperated sigh. "Because fishnets and a thong are not the best to travel in." She rolled her eyes as if I should have known that.

"Fishnets and thongs? What'd I miss?" Drake chuckled as he walked into the kitchen. He took the spot on the other side of Piper, so close that her back stiffened. Drake leaned in to whisper in her ear. "Please tell me you will be wearing them?"

Piper's face brightened to a pretty shade of pink and turned to smack Drake on the shoulder. "Stop it. And I'm not wearing it for you. I'm wearing it for Wynn." The atmosphere of the room grew tense. "It's all for Wynn. Everything I do is for him. To get him back." Her eyes drifted over to Darren, something passing between them. I wanted to know what.

Except that didn't matter right now. What mattered was doing what Antoine ordered me to do no matter how much I was against it.

"Before we go up to your room and you show me exactly what you plan on wearing—" Piper opened her mouth to argue with me, but I covered her lips with my hand. "I know you have a hard time keeping your mouth shut, but for the moment, you need to listen to me. And listen good."

Piper's breath was hot against my palm, but she nodded. I lowered my hand and waited to see if she would interrupt me. When she didn't, I continued, "Now, I'm sure you've been told what to expect at Club Dead, but there is more to it than just how you look. It's how you act."

Her hands on her hips, she stared me down. "What's wrong with how I act?"

Drake snorted and shook his head. "Remember when Valentine visited the first time?"

Piper went dead silent, her heartbeat pounding in my ears. Realizing what was going on, I glared at Drake over her shoulder, swiping my hand across my neck. Drake's brows furrowed, apparently not getting the twin signals I was sending his way. Huffing, I gave up, throwing my hands in the air. I sat them on Piper's arms, rubbing them up and down in a soothing manner. "It's okay. You're fine. He's gone."

Drake stared at us in confusion. "What did I say?"

I narrowed my eyes on my other half and pushed him away from Piper. To Darren, I asked, "Can we get some tea for Piper?"

Darren inclined his head, turning to the stove to put the kettle on.

"I don't like tea," Piper murmured, lifting her head to meet my gaze. Her pupils were dilated but her breathing had slowed, and her heartbeat was back to a regular rhythm.

"Chamomile. It'll help," I reassured her, stepping back to give her some space. "Are you alright?"

Nodding, she slid into a stool at the island. Darren placed a cup in front of her, dropping a bag of chamomile in.

Drake finally seemed to figure out where he went wrong. His eyes went tight and then he rubbed a hand down his face with a groan. "Fuck. Piper, I'm sorry. I didn't realize. I mean, I didn't mean—"

"It's fine," Piper snapped, not looking away from the cup in front of her. She played with the tea bag, dipping it up and down in the cup, even though it didn't have any water. "You were saying something about how I should act?"

Seeing she wanted to change the subject, I sat down on the stool next to her. "The way you had to act before, seen but not heard?" She nodded numbly. "Forget all that. It doesn't apply at the club." I paused while Darren poured hot water into Piper's cup. Piper continued fiddling with the bag as if nothing had happened. I placed my hand on her shoulder, waiting until she looked up at me. "This is serious, Piper."

"I'm listening." Piper lifted her cup to her mouth, taking small sips.

"You can't just walk around on your own. You have to stay by one of us at all times. Preferably Antoine, since he's your master."

Piper choked on the tea, coughing it up as she sat her cup down. "What?"

I frowned, my brows drawing together. "What part? The standing by one of us?"

"The master bit," Drake pointed out with a wicked grin. "I don't think Piper could think of any of us as her master."

Piper shook her head, a smile finally creeping over her face. "No, not in this lifetime."

Pressing my lips into a thin line, I gave them both a stern look. "Regardless, you must pretend like Antoine has some kind of hold over you. The others, the vampires, need to know who you belong to." Piper snorted into her cup, I ignored it and continued, "Like it or not, as Antoine's human servant, you belong to him. They need to think you belong to him." I was really trying to drill it in. "You shouldn't talk to anyone without consulting Antoine."

"And if Antoine isn't there?" Piper swiveled in her seat, finally paying full attention to me. "What do I do then? Pretend to be mute?"

Drake clamped his hand on her shoulder, turning her gaze to him. "Then you find one of us and you never leave with anyone."

Taking her chin in my hand, I shifted it back to me. "No one. Only us. These vampires aren't like us or even Boris who at least pretends to be civilized, even though he's a treacherous shark. These vampires don't care who you are or who you belong to. They only respond to power. If you don't have anyone there to protect you then it's—"

"Open season," Drake finished for me, chomping his teeth menacingly.

"Don't let your guard down even for a second," I told her, just as Rayne came into the kitchen.

"You don't have to worry about that. Piper's guard is never down." Rayne's eyes narrowed on the pretty maid before he headed to the fridge.

Piper frowned at him then turned back to her tea. "Don't mind him. He's still pissed that I used sex to distract him so I could come to Savannah."

I eyed the back of Rayne's head while he searched the fridge. When he pulled out his silver container of blood, he didn't even bother to heat it up. He turned and leaned against the counter next to Darren, who watched with all the interest of a statue. Rayne spun the lid off and drank deeply from the container, his eyes on Piper the whole time. If looks could kill...

Drake chortled and wrapped an arm around Piper's waist, pulling her to his side. "Just so it's out there, you can use sex to distract me any time."

Sighing at the amount of drama that had come to our household, I turned back to Piper. "Now, about your outfit."

Chapter 8
Piper

AFTER A TWO-HOUR limo ride and one gas stop later, we were in front of Club Dead. Dark red brick covered the front of the building with blacked out windows and a metal front door. There wasn't even a line to get in.

"Not what you expected?"

I jumped in my seat by the window and glanced back at Drake, who'd sat next to me the whole ride, helping Allister prep me for tonight. I knew far too much about vampire politics than I ever wanted to know.

Like keep my eyes down. Don't make direct eye contact with anyone, it would be seen as an invitation. Keep within arm distance of one of them at all times. Allow

Antoine to touch me as much as he wanted and never push him away. It would be a show of weakness for him if his human servant didn't even want to be with him.

I just hoped Antoine didn't toe the line of my sanity the way he had with Darren in his office. My eyes flicked to the front of the limo where Darren sat behind a removable divider.

Everything that happened in the office was so confusing. Not the part where I had to prove myself, I understood why Antoine did it, but why did Darren? I'd been worried about whether or not he had really consented or if he'd only been doing what he was told. Also, there was that insecure part of me that needed to know we were okay. That we hadn't ruined our friendship.

To my utter dismay and relief, Darren hadn't changed how he acted around me at all. It was as if his dick had never been inside me. Maybe I was thinking too much about it.

"You are." Rayne's voice came from the seat next to the divider, interrupting my thoughts, making me realize I'd been staring at the front of the limo for a long time, having never answered Drake's question.

Realizing Rayne had just read my mind, my face flushed. "Stop that."

"Don't project so much," Rayne countered, shifting in his seat, his arms crossed over his mostly bare chest.

When the guys had told me the club was different, they hadn't been kidding. Every single one of them were decked out like regular club hoppers, naughty club hoppers. Rayne wore shiny leather pants that clung to every inch of him, his torso only covered by a white fishnet top. I'd had to pick my jaw up off the floor the moment I saw him because I was drooling so much. Thankfully, my reaction had softened his anger toward me somewhat. I hated for us to go into this fighting. I was doing it all for Wynn. I didn't want to lose Rayne too.

"What am I missing here?" Drake, clad in dark washed, ripped jeans and a ribbed, neon green tank top, paired with black combat boots, frowned, his gaze jerking between Rayne and me.

Allister, who was dressed similarly to his brother, except his tank top was blue, leaned into our conversation as well. "I've been wondering that the whole way here. Something's going on with you three."

Marcus was the only one of our group who was missing. He had some things to check into, other contacts to question about Wynn's location. I was glad for his absence with the focus all on me. Except, we might need his help later.

I pulled my lower lip between my teeth, worrying it while I tried to figure out what to say. Did I just flat out tell them Darren and I had sex...or sort of? I didn't know if Darren would want them to know or if it was something that had just been between us three—well, four now, since Rayne had apparently read my mind.

Honestly, I was surprised he hadn't freaked out about it. I mean, I'd hopped out of bed with him only to get into it—or on the desk with—Darren and then Antoine. He'd already established he was fine with sharing with his brother, but Darren? We hadn't really talked about it.

Rayne grunted and knocked his knuckles against the divider. The divider buzzed as it lowered, revealing the driver and Darren.

"Yes, Master Rayne?" Darren turned to peer into the backseat. His eyes darted to me for a brief second before landing on Rayne.

"Do you feel like your rights have been violated in anyway?" Rayne asked, making the twins perk up with interest and me want to sink into the floor and die.

Darren's gaze shifted to Antoine, who had been particularly quiet during this ride. He was one of the only ones who hadn't changed

92

much. Gone was the suit jacket, but he wore black slacks and a blood-red, button-down shirt with the first three buttons undone, showing off the house sigil over his heart. He'd braided his pale hair, which hung over one shoulder, and added diamond stud earrings that gave him a rakish quality. He looked like something out of a romance novel that had me wanting to stay home and play damsel in distress.

Antoine moved his gaze from the window to Darren, giving a little flick of his hand in his direction.

Apparently, that was all the permission Darren needed to spill the beans. Those dark orbs locked on to me and his lips twitched slightly as he raked his gaze over my body, and murmured, "No. They have not." The need in his eyes caused heat to pool between my thighs, making the tiny, neon blue leather skirt I wore feel like nothing at all. The bright blue fishnets I'd placed under them did nothing to hide my arousal as it filled the car. The vampires around me inhaled deeply, and a low rumbling came from Drake beside me.

"Now I really think we've missed something." Drake's voice had taken on a growl, his swirling, cerulean eyes moving over to me, or more like my lap, and then to the heavy cleavage showing through the white halter top I wore. I'd forgone a bra to wear it, my nipples stiffening against the fabric, no doubt visible through the thin material.

Allister had barely approved my outfit. One I'd had from a few Halloween's ago when I actually had a semblance of a social life. Apparently, it wasn't quite racy enough. Though, unless they wanted me to go in there naked, I didn't know what else I was supposed to wear. Darren hadn't had to dress up like this. He had on his normal butler attire, including the white gloves. When I'd protested, Allister scoffed, "They know him."

Like that was all I needed to know. So, apparently, I had to be with them for several centuries before I could not show my ass.

"So..." Rayne, once more interrupting my spiral of thoughts, pushed out of his seat and edged toward the door. "Now that we have established everyone is good. Can we get in there? If Piper gets any more turned on, I don't think we're ever getting inside, and then this was all for nothing."

The divider went back up and the front limo door opened and shut. Footsteps came to the back of the limo and both doors opened at the same time. Antoine slipped out one side with Rayne close behind him. I stepped a foot out of the limo, but Drake grabbed my arm, with Allister still in the limo behind him.

"What?" I arched a brow, anxious to get inside and get this over with.

Drake gave me a serious look, something I'd rarely seen from him. "Did you and Darren...?" He trailed off, expecting me to fill in the blanks.

Against my will, my cheeks heated, and I turned my face away from them. "Uh, yeah."

Drake swore, banging his hand on the side of the limo. "Even the butler is further ahead of the game than us." He elbowed his brother who rolled his eyes. "We're losing our touch, brother."

Allister's matching cerulean eyes drifted over me, my skin tingling where his gaze touched. "No, we're not."

Shaking my head clear of the fog that'd rolled in, I withdrew from Drake's grasp, sauntering over to Antoine and Darren in my one pair of stiletto heels. While Darren didn't have to touch Antoine or even be near him—another perk of being with him for so long—I had to stay within touching distance. Antoine didn't even glance my way when his arm slid around my waist, riding low on my hip.

"Nervous?" Antoine inquired, while we waited for the twins to catch up.

I started to shake my head, but Antoine caught my eye and I stopped, murmuring, "Petrified."

"Good. You should be." Antoine's eyes hardened on the metal door before us. "Maybe it will keep you from getting into trouble."

Rayne snort laughed, and I glared at him over my shoulder. "I can stay out of trouble."

Smirking at me, his voice patronizing, Rayne said, "Sure you can, babe."

I spun around in Antoine's arm and flipped him off just as Darren knocked on the metal door before us. Antoine's hand squeezed my hip and I twisted back around quickly, while Rayne guffawed at my expense. A pair of eyes appeared in the little window of the door. They scanned over our group before snapping the window shut with a clank. The door opened seconds later. Apparently, they knew who we were.

My hands grew damp and I tried to wipe them off on my skirt, but the leather material made it impossible. I could barely hear the music pouring out of the club over the pounding of my heart, my breathing coming in short, fast pants.

Antoine's head angled toward me, his lips at my ear. "Relax." His power rushed through me, and instantly I felt better. I took a deep breath and lifted my gaze to his. "Better?"

I nodded. "Yes, thank you."

"Thank you what?"

My eyes darted around the long, narrow hallway, illuminated only by red lights. The others had already gone ahead, leaving Antoine and I alone in the hallway. Licking my lips, I shifted closer to him. If I was going to play the willing little human servant, I was going to play it to the best of my ability. Pushing up on my tiptoes, I grasped the sides of his shirt and leaned in until my breath brushed against his lips. "Yes, master."

The hand on my waist dipped down and cupped my backside, fingers brushing the thong beneath while his other hand clasped the back of my neck. Without warning, he took my lips in a brutal kiss, shoving his tongue into my mouth. I arched into him, rubbing my breasts against him as I took everything he gave me.

A sharp pain sliced through my lip and I jerked back with a wince. "Ouch. What'd you do that for?" I probed at the small slice on my lip. It barely bled, but it still hurt like a bitch.

Antoine released my neck and brushed his thumb across my lower lip. "So, they know who you belong to."

A weird kind of warmth filled my chest at his words. While I'd never really ever call Antoine master—women's rights and all—knowing that he thought of me as his made something girly and feminine bubble in my stomach. Apparently, my feelings were leaking over to Antoine, because the bastard smiled knowingly before taking me by the waist once more and steering us down the hallway.

The music grew louder the farther we went, the beat a sultry but pulsating rhythm that made my body want to writhe to it. The hallway ended on a turn, bringing us right into the thick of things. A bar sat along the right side of a dance floor, its bartenders handing out more red drinks than anything else. Bodies rubbed and wriggled on the dance floor, most of them practically dry humping each other. As my eyes took in the outfits of the people around me, I realized mine was the tamest one here. Lifted sections with poles in the middle of them had women in thongs and pasties, while the others on the dance floor all wore some form of lingerie. A few sparse ones wore tight fitted dresses that barely covered their asses, but overall I felt highly overdressed.

The men weren't an exception. My guys fit in, but they were far from the norm where clothing was concerned. Most of the men went shirtless, a few even wore thongs as well, but one thing I noticed over all the others were the vampires. It was easy to see who was a vampire and who wasn't. Those who were vampires didn't bare their skin for everyone to see. At least, not as much. It was the humans that showed off the most flesh. Some of them showing even more than was needed as they sat with their companions in some of the booths and low lounge chairs.

My mouth parted as I caught sight of a male vampire with his fangs deep in the neck of another man, his hand groping him under the tabletop. No one seemed to be bothered by it or tried to stop them. In fact, the longer I looked around, my mind registering what it saw, the more people I noticed in similar positions. Having been fucked and bitten at the same time before, and enjoying the sight of it, gave me mixed feelings.

Desire pulsated between my thighs and fear skittered through my veins. My body didn't know what it wanted to do, how I should react, and I had a feeling that this was just the beginning.

Drake and Allister stood off to the side at the bar, a drink already in their hands. Rayne sat at a table a few yards away, waving off women who flocked to him the instant he sat down. Pride swelled in my chest knowing he was mine. Those amber eyes locked on to mine and a crooked smile teased his lips.

Antoine's hand tightened slightly on my waist, pulling my attention back to him. "I'm going to go find Morpheus so we can get this over with. Stay with the twins or Rayne."

"Not Darren?" I lifted a brow, wondering if he was still jealous.

"Darren belongs at my side." I opened my mouth to argue that I was his human servant too, but he gave me a stern look that reminded me of where we were. "Please behave while I'm gone." He gave me another toe tingling kiss that drew the gazes of several vampires and humans alike before passing me off to Drake and Allister. Drake handed me a glass with something pink and fizzy in it. I took it gratefully, downing half of it in one go.

Drake chuckled and wrapped his arm around my shoulders, steering me toward the table where Rayne waited. "Well, Miss Billings, you wanted to be a part of our world." He gestured around with his glass. "Welcome to Club Dead."

Chapter 9
Rayne

WATCHING PIPER'S FACE AND hearing her thoughts as she took in Club Dead was like being there for the first time. Even my first time had been something out of a dark and twisted fairy tale. I'd only been changed for a little bit. Five years, I think. Wynn was the one who took me. Antoine didn't like anyone to come near vampire masters unless they had to, which I fully understood now. Antoine had to save Wynn and me the last time we came. What they had to do to leave...it haunted me even now.

I shuddered as I imagined what Morpheus might make us or Piper do to get the information we needed.

"You okay?" Piper glanced away from the dance floor to me. Though she wasn't supposed to be looking around, she couldn't seem to help herself. However, she was drawing far too much attention. I already counted five vampires who had noticed her, and none of their thoughts were pleasant.

I'd like to sink my fangs into that rack.

Wonder if she would scream?

The Durands are so fucking hot. I bet that little slut is fucking all of them.

And on and on it went. Places like this were killer on my head. I couldn't block out all of the thoughts, and it made it impossible to concentrate on what was in front of me.

"Rayne?" Piper shook my arm, jerking me back to our table. "Are you alright?" She placed a hand on the side of my face, concern etched across her features.

I kissed her palm and nodded. "Yeah, just a bit overwhelmed."

Piper giggled, sipping her pretty pink drink. "I know what you mean. This place is...wow." She gestured around, her eyes wide and full of wonder. *How many of these people want to be here?*

Good. While I wanted her to have fun, I didn't want her to forget that she was in a club full of vampires willing and waiting to rip her throat out. I couldn't handle it if anything happened to her.

"I'm telling you," Drake's voice grew louder as he argued with his twin, "there's no way you can get her away from Lucas." He gestured his head toward the table across the way where a busty blonde, wearing pink hot pants and a strip of cloth across her breasts that didn't even count as clothing, giggled at something her vampire companion said.

Lucas, a three-century old vampire with a small dick—Wynn's words, not mine—had a bad temper, but a remarkable way with the ladies, and that was even without any exceptional powers. Lucas wore his brown hair short and styled on top, and his nose was crooked from being in one too many fights before he became a vampire. He had a scar that went through one eyebrow, which also had to have been predeath. The women found him dangerous and charming, two things that were a volatile combination—I knew from the fact that he never stopped thinking about how pretty the blonde would look with her throat ripped open and her blood coating him.

"I think you should try," I told Allister with a knowing look. "If you don't, she won't live through the night."

Drake's and Allister's expressions hardened, both of their gazes going pointedly to Lucas's table. Piper watched on with a horrified expression. I could tell she wanted to help her too, but thankfully she firmly stayed in place and watched the twins get up from the table.

They strolled across the dance floor, several humans, men and women, trying to garner their attention as they went. They ignored them though, their eyes only on the blonde. When they reached Lucas's table, it wasn't hard to tell what was going on. Drake did his usual jockish thing, being overconfident and making her flush red. He wasn't even using his powers on her, which said more about him than it did Lucas.

Lucas didn't stand a chance when Allister put on the charm as well. *Both at once? Oh, God yes!* The blonde barely thought it before jumping out of her seat and latching on to both twins' arms.

Lucas stood up, his brows furrowed and teeth gnashing as he said something to them that couldn't be heard over the loud music. Part of why it was played so loudly.

Drake shook his head at him before turning away. Lucas apparently didn't like that and swung at him. Drake ducked and swiped his leg out, knocking Lucas's legs out from under him and tumbling him onto his back. Drake's hand wrapped around Lucas's throat, keeping him pinned to the ground. The blonde only watched on with a happy glee at having the vampires fight over her.

"What's going on?" Piper whispered near my ear. "Is she going to be okay?"

I nodded. "Yeah. Lucas is a dick, but he's not suicidal. We might not come here often, but most people know who we are and not to fuck with us," I said matter-of-factly, without a single ounce of pride. The majority of the fear for our family came from being Boris's creatures and not from being our own house. Double-edged sword, that one.

Turning back into my seat as the twins brought their new friend over, I slipped an arm around Piper's shoulders. Piper leaned into my embrace, not questioning my motives at all. While I loved having Piper pressed against me, the move was to make sure the blonde didn't get any ideas about a foursome. I shared, but not that much. Besides, I didn't think Piper would be too keen on that.

The twins returned to our table with the giggling blonde in tow. Allister slid into the booth first, pressing up against Piper's other side. Drake sat down next to them, leaving the blonde in front of the table. Cami was the name I picked from her brain. She was twenty-one and wanted nothing more than to have a vampire bite and fuck her. Well, she'd come to the right place.

"This is Cami," Drake introduced her with a wink, taking her hand in his. Cami giggled once more, not seeming bothered by the lack of chairs for her. She promptly placed herself on the table in front of Drake and Allister, one leg in each of their laps.

Twisting to the side, she glanced over at me with lust in her eyes before they landed on Piper. Her brows drew down, her thoughts turned to jealousy, but then Drake slid a hand up the inside of her thigh and she was over it.

Piper couldn't tear her gaze away from her and the twins. While they weren't touching her in any inappropriate places, it was clear they intended to feed on her. It made me curious how Piper would react. I knew the twins had been vying for her attention, but I wasn't sure biting another woman in front of Piper was going to win her affections.

"So, Cami," Allister murmured, his voice heavy with his powers, making Cami shudder in need. "Why did you come here tonight?"

I held back a snort at his question. We could all smell why she came here tonight.

You could scent the arousal on her like a heavy perfume. Piper wasn't even dense enough not to see it. As far as Cami was concerned, she thought she'd won the jackpot.

Cami knew how to play right into the vampires' clutches though. No way she was a first timer. Leaning her head to the side, her legs spreading ever so slightly, she breathed out, "To see you of course."

The twins exchanged a look and they seemed to settle on something without making a sound or thought. Drake stood slightly, pressing her thighs to the side of his hips, his hand coming up to tangle in her short blonde locks. Allister shifted until he was between her legs, spreading them as wide as they would go. Cami's breath hitched as Allister's finger trailed along her femoral artery.

I glanced over to the side. Piper sat on the edge of her seat as she watched them take their positions. A small inhale told me all I needed to know about how she felt in this moment. Watching the twins sink their teeth into Cami wasn't something she found disgusting or horrendous. She was turned on, a lot. Slipping into her mind for a second, I was shocked by what I saw there.

Piper was jealous, not because she hated that they were touching Cami, but because she wanted to *be* Cami. She wanted the twins to do what they were doing to the blonde woman to her.

My lips ticked up in amusement. Perhaps Piper was made for my brothers and me after all. If only Marcus could get the stick out of his ass. Not likely.

I wasn't the only one who noticed Piper's arousal. Allister's hooded gaze locked on to Piper over the edge of Cami's thigh, where he drank deeply from her. For Piper's benefit, Allister stroked along Cami's thigh, down her calf, and back up. Piper's breathing grew faster the longer she watched, until Drake seemed to catch on as well.

Changing sides, Drake sank his fangs back into Cami's neck, all the while watching Piper. Unlike his brother, who at least had some class, Drake slid his hand down Cami's back and grabbed a handful of her ass, making the woman moan.

Piper downed the rest of her drink and pushed at my side. "Uh, let's dance."

Chuckling at her obvious need for an escape, I winked at my brothers before leading Piper to the dance floor. Cami didn't even notice our departure. Not that I expected her to, but I knew my brothers would leave her satisfied and alive, which was all that mattered.

A slow thumping beat played over the large speakers. I thought Piper would flounder, since she didn't seem the type to have any rhythm. She tripped over her own feet so much that she was an insurance hazard all on her own. However, when we arrived on the dance floor, she turned her back to me, her hands up as she swayed from side to side.

Like a snake in a trance, I moved closer to her, pressing my front to her back. My hands settled on her hips, moving to the music with her. Piper's hands reached back and tangled in my hair, drawing me closer. My cock hardened against the stimulation, and if I didn't know any better, I'd think she was purposely rubbing her ass over it. When she let out a long, drawn out moan, I knew she was.

"You're going to get me in trouble, babe," I whispered into her ear, pressing a kiss to the side of her neck. "We're supposed to be keeping a lookout for Marcus or Antoine, not having foreplay on the dance floor."

Piper's grin could be heard through her words as she asked, "Who said we can't do both?"

My hand drifted from her hip to her lower belly, and I felt her heart jump at my touch. "Tell me, if I bent you over and took you right here on the dance floor, would you stop me?"

Spinning around, Piper wrapped her arms around my neck and pressed her front to mine, her nipples rubbing against my bare chest beneath my fishnet top. Her lips brushed mine as she ground herself against me. *Try it and find out.*

I frowned. Something was off.

Pulling my mouth away from Piper's, I ignored the confusion on her face and searched the room with my mind. This wasn't like Piper. Piper would have blushed and stuttered before going to hide in the bathroom. Then there was the fact that Antoine hadn't come back yet. He should have been back by now.

Just a little more, I heard a voice hiss in my mind. A moment later, another body pressed against the back of Piper— a vampire I didn't recognize. His long, black hair was pulled back tight into a ponytail, and the vampire had at least a foot on me in height. His greedy hands landed on Piper's hips and she leaned into him, not bothered by the stranger. She released her grip on me and writhed against the new vampire. *That's it. Morpheus will be pleased.*

I grabbed for her, trying to get her away from him. "Hey, that's my date."

The stranger flashed his fangs and me, pushing me away. "Not anymore."

Piper didn't even notice that I'd been shoved away. She moaned and wiggled even closer to the vampire. Piper angled her head to the side, something she wouldn't have done for anyone but one of us. Not giving the vampire a chance to sink his fangs into my girlfriend, I grabbed on to his ponytail and yanked hard. The vampire turned away from Piper with a hiss, his fangs bared at me.

"It's rude to try and take another person's human," I snapped, wrapping the ponytail around my hand until the vampire's head strained to the side.

He struggled against my hold, but while he might be bigger, I was older. There was no way he could beat me. "Can't take what's freely given."

"Didn't look that way to me," Drake growled, appearing with Allister at his side. "I smell power and not yours. Who's your master?"

Allister grabbed Piper before she could be taken by one of the several vampires who had begun to crowd around us. None of them looked friendly and I was beginning to think this was planned.

"Morpheus," I bit out, jerking the vampire down to the ground. "Where is he?"

The vampires around us laughed.

"You won't be seeing him tonight. Or ever, for that matter," one of them taunted. Drake whipped around and kicked the vampire in the chest, sending him flying. Humans screamed and darted for the doors. Vampires sat and watched, more interested in the fight than leaving with their lives. Fucking idiots.

As if an invisible signal had been given, the vampires around us attacked. I kicked the vampire in my hands in the face, knocking him out just as a pair of hands wrapped around my waist. They hauled me back, more hands grabbing at me. I searched their minds as I lashed out. Punching a vampire in the face, I wasted no time jerking my head back to hit the one holding me in the nose. I heard a crunch and a groan before the arms dropped away. The image of being punched in the face hit my mind milliseconds before I ducked. The fist that had been meant for me hit one of their friends instead.

While I was busy with my assailants, I couldn't keep an eye on my brothers or Piper. I knew they could take care of themselves, but with Piper there as well, I wasn't so sure she would make it out alive.

As if sensing my fears, Piper's scream pierced through the room. I kneed a vampire in the stomach before placing both hands on the sides of his neck, twisting until flesh ripped. Dropping the head on the ground, I shoved through the remaining vampires, zeroing in on Piper.

Three vampires were surrounding her, and Allister was overwhelmed by another three, unable to help her. I cursed and yelled over my shoulder, "Drake, your brother!"

Drake punched the vampire he was fighting in the face and searched for his brother. When he found him, he saluted. "Got it. You get Piper."

The spell Piper had been under seemed to have broken as she fought and clawed at the vampires trying to take a bite out of her. I grabbed the back of the neck of the one going in for the kill and threw him over my shoulder. The two holding her arms dropped her to face me. I grabbed Piper around the waist and pulled her to me. "I got you. You're safe."

"Not for long, Morpheus wants her," one of the vampires said, licking his lips. "And what the boss wants, he gets."

"Not this time," I snapped, prepared to fight once more.

Releasing Piper, I dove for the first guy, kicking him in the knees. A loud crack, followed by his howls of pain, brought him down in a second. The other vampire wasn't so easy to fight off. This one was a lot older and his arms were like a vise that wrapped around my neck as he tried to rip my head off. Piper screamed, the vampire I'd gotten off her before coming after her again.

"Piper!" I reached out for her, struggling against the hold on me, but I couldn't break free. I watched helplessly as the vampire grabbed Piper and opened his mouth, ready to sink his fangs into her.

Suddenly, the vampire stopped mid-strike. His eyes widened and a squelching sound came before he fell forward, right onto a screaming Piper. Marcus appeared behind the vampire, his hand covered in blood, the vampire's heart in his hand. His dark eyes glared down at the dead vampire before hauling him off of Piper. Piper scrambled up from the ground and threw herself at a stunned Marcus.

With Piper safe, I could focus on my own fight. Using a power I knew would wear me down, I shoved my mind inside the vampire holding me, overloading him with images. His arms loosened around me before dropping completely as he clutched his skull, howling as he scratched at his head unable to fight the pain. I kept it up until he was dead on the ground, his eyes bleeding with long, deep grooves down the sides of his face.

"Ew." Piper gagged, gripping my arm as she stared down at the vampire. "I didn't know you could do that."

"I don't do it often because—" I didn't get the words out before I stumbled from the weight of exhaustion pressing down on me. Piper caught me, keeping me up on my feet.

"Marcus!" Piper called out, surprising me again that she called to him for help over the twins.

I couldn't focus on the thought as my mind threatened to darken. Thick, strong arms wrapped around my waist and I was hauled up. A wrist was shoved against my lips and blood touched my mouth. Recognizing Marcus's blood, I greedily bit down. I drank until my mind cleared and then pushed his wrist away.

"Thanks." I wiped the blood from my lips and frowned at Marcus. "Took you long enough."

"I was delayed." Marcus looked away from us, toward the office Antoine had disappeared into. "Now let's go find our brother."

Chapter 10
Antoine

"MORPHEUS," I GROWLED, MY patience already running on fumes. "We have toasted to our health, to the kingdom of vampires, and to the bloody president's well-being. We have discussed the state of your city and mine, but what we haven't discussed is what I came here for." I sat my wine glass on the table between us and stood. "Now, since it seems like you don't have any information of importance for getting my brother back, then I'll be leaving. You understand the urgency of the situation."

"I grasp it quite well. I just don't see what the hurry is. He's not going anywhere. Not while he's with your master." Morpheus's bright green eyes gleamed over his glass, a Cheshire-like grin on his lips.

Darren stood at my back, a step behind my chair, quiet and unassuming as he should be. If I thought Piper could keep her mouth shut for a goddamn minute, I'd have let her come with me, but now that I knew this was all a waste of time, I was regretting bringing any of them at all.

Morpheus's human servant sat on a cushion on the floor by Morpheus's feet. A degrading position, if there ever was one. She was a pretty woman who couldn't be above the age of sixteen, with bright blue eyes and auburn hair. She kept her gaze on the ground, her neck and arms littered with bite marks. A good master would heal her wounds, but Morpheus had never been known to be a good master, let alone vampire.

"You're wasting my time and my patience." I adjusted my sleeves before turning toward the door. "Come, Darren. We're leaving."

Morpheus stood, his chair scratching the ground from the force. " Don't be so hasty. I have the information you want."

I spun around and narrowed my eyes on him, pushing power into my voice. "Then give it to me so I can leave."

Cocking his head to the side, Morpheus gave me a fang toothed grin. "Now who is being rude? Using your powers on your host? Someone who is trying to help you out of the goodness of his heart?"

I pressed my lips into a thin line. "You're doing this out of something, but your heart? Doubtful."

A small smile played on Morpheus's lips as he picked up his wine glass to pour it into a metal dish on the small, circular table before placing it on the floor by the girl. The girl dashed for the dish like a starved animal, and from the way her clothes hung on her form, that was likely to be the case. "Can't I want to spend some time with an old friend?"

Stepping toward the table, I placed my hand on the back of the chair. "Forgive me. I am simply desperate to get Wynn back."

Morpheus nodded in understanding, his hand gesturing to the chair. "Please have a seat. Even if you get the information I have, you can't do anything about it tonight. You might as well enjoy yourself while you're here." A sly grin slid up his lips. "Just as your brothers and your new human servant are right now. Piper, isn't it?"

My back stiffened at the mention of Piper. "Leave them out of this. This is between you and me. What do you want?"

"Oh, no, Antoine. I do not think you are in any position to be giving me demands." Morpheus picked up the bottle of wine sitting between us and poured himself another glass, as well as filling mine. "I'll tell you what you want to know when I'm good and ready and not before."

Gritting my teeth, I picked up my glass and lifted it to my lips. Before I could take a drink, the door to the office burst open. Marcus and the rest of the household poured into the room, beat up and bleeding. Piper's halter top had been torn, tear stains streaking her face.

"Antoine." Marcus marched to my side, his eyes narrowing on Morpheus. "It was an ambush."

Seeing that I'd been delayed for nothing other than trickery, my hand tightened around my glass until it shattered in my grip. I didn't even feel the shards cutting into my palm. "What is the meaning of this, Morpheus? I come into your club as you requested. I have been nothing if not patient, and the way you repay me is by attacking my family?" My whole body vibrated with the need for violence as I stared Morpheus down. The bastard didn't even seem bothered by the fact he had been found out or that he was surrounded. In fact, he practically beamed with delight.

"It seems the rumors are true." Morpheus lifted his glass to his lips, one leg crossing over the other as his gaze ran over my group. "You have been a busy little vampire, Antoine. Your household could rival that of your master's."

"He's no master of ours," Rayne bit out, taking a step forward.

I held my hand up, holding him back. "Is that what this was? A test of strength? If so, then you have your answer. Now give me what I came for."

Morpheus clucked his tongue, his eyes drifting over to Piper. "Now, now, what's the rush? You've defeated my children, there's no threat here."

"Think again." Drake curled his fingers into a fist, pounding it against the palm of his other hand.

Laughing in delight, Morpheus shifted his gaze back to me. "I will give you what you want, but I want something in return."

"Of course you do." I lifted my hand, gesturing to Darren. He gave me my checkbook without a word, bowing deeply. "How much, Morpheus?"

"How much what?" the bastard echoed cheekily, his eyes never straying from Piper.

"Money." I tried to hold back my sigh of annoyance. He was drawing this out on purpose, and I was seconds away from ripping his heart out and saying fuck it to whatever information he might have.

A gleam appeared in Morpheus's eyes. "I don't want your money." He lifted his arms, his wine glass in hand, gesturing around him. "Do I look like I need it?"

Handing my checkbook back to Darren, I leveled a neutral look on him. "Then what do you want?"

"Her." He dipped his wine glass to Piper. "I'll even trade you." He snapped his fingers and the girl crawled over to him so he could place his hand on her head. "Patrice has been broken in and doesn't mind being shared. Do you, dear?"

Patrice's hollowed face never changed expression as her head bobbed up and down. She seemed to have lost all will to fight. Nothing showed behind her eyes. No fear. No excitement. Only blankness.

I bared my fangs at him, reaching across the table to grab his shirt in my hands. "You insult me, Morpheus. One cannot simply trade human servants like they are property to barter."

Morpheus's brows drew together, a tight frown on his lips. "That is where you are wrong, my old friend. You might have strengthened your household, but you have gone soft over the years. Humans are for food and maybe the occasional fuck but nothing else, and here you prioritize your human over Wynn. Your own blood brother. You're a disgrace to vampires everywhere."

"Be that as it may, I will not give you Piper." I shoved him, releasing his shirt and knocking him back into his seat. "Pick something else."

Morpheus seemed to think it over and then angled his head to the side. "Then a taste. If I cannot have her, let me taste her."

Rayne sucked in a sharp breath. "No. No way. Not happening. Antoine, you can't let him do this."

"Yeah," Allister agreed, moving to my side as well. "She's still recovering from—"

I held up a hand, not wanting him to reveal any more. "I do not need you to tell me what I need to do." My eyes locked on to Morpheus, and I pressed my lips into a firm line. "I will not let you taste her. Piper is new to the ways of vampires. I would not have you break her so soon."

Morpheus did not like my answer. His eyes flared with anger and his jaw tightened as the hand on Patrice's head clenched her hair, making the poor girl squeak from pain.

"Fine. Then give me him for the night. The redhead." Morpheus jerked his chin toward Rayne.

Piper made the first sound since coming into the room, playing the dutiful human servant perfectly. The small, startled cry that slipped through her lips was so soft, it wouldn't have been noticed by anyone other than a vampire. That small sound caused Morpheus's lips to curl up into a wicked grin.

"That is my final offer. Either a taste of your new human servant or a night with the boy." Morpheus released his grip on Patrice's hair, lacing his fingers together over his stomach. "The choice is yours."

"It is not my choice to make," I announced, turning in my seat to meet Rayne's gaze. *Rayne?*

To the untrained eye, one would not think Morpheus's request bothered Rayne, but I knew what Rayne had been through before. What he'd been subjected to. I wasn't about to make this decision for him. Not with the way the muscle in his cheek twitched.

When Rayne took a step forward, Piper grabbed his arm, dropping all pretenses. "No, Rayne. No. You can't do this."

"I can." Rayne stared down at her with a sad smile on his lips. "For Wynn, right?"

Piper shook her head, pulling him back. "No, I won't let you. He can taste me. Take me instead."

"Well, well, isn't this an interesting turn of events." Morpheus grinned from ear to ear, leaning on the arm of his chair as if watching a particularly thrilling movie. "The broken vampire or the fragile human. Whoever will come out on top?"

"Piper." Allister took her by the arm and drew her to the side. "You don't understand what you're asking. It won't be like with Valentine. Morpheus will make it hurt."

Narrowing her eyes on Allister, she jerked her arm away. "Do you think what he did to me didn't hurt?"

Sighing with frustration, Allister placed his hands on her shoulders. "This won't be the same. What Valentine did was out of anger, what Morpheus will do will be out of pleasure. He likes to hurt women." He gestured to Patrice on the floor. "Do you think she enjoyed any of those bites? While I don't like the idea of letting Rayne being with him," he winced as he looked over at our youngest brother, "he, I know, will bounce back from it. You might not and we can't lose you after Wynn's sacrifice."

"Aaahhh." Morpheus smirked and chuckled. "I wondered how slippery Wynn had ended up in the hands of your master. Now I see." I wanted to scoop his eyes out with a spoon for the way he leered at Piper.

Later, I told myself. We needed the information on Wynn's whereabouts. I could torture him for this later.

Piper pushed Allister's hands off of her, patting him on the chest. "Thank you for worrying over me, but that's precisely why I have to do this." Shifting away from Allister, she straightened her back and walked toward the table. Rayne reached for her, but she must have thought something because he dropped his hand, his face the picture of pure agony.

Stopping at my side, Piper lifted her chin. "Tell us where Wynn is."

Morpheus stood from his chair and practically ran Patrice over in his hurry to get to Piper. "You have no idea how ecstatic I am for your decision, my dear. It is quite brave and selfless of you."

"Stop patronizing her and tell us what we want to know. Then and only then will you get your payment," I bit out, gesturing to Marcus.

He moved forward to stand behind Piper, his arms crossed over his chest, glowering down at Morpheus.

"And Marcus here will make sure you do not overstep yourself," I explained, as if all of this was just business now. I didn't want him to know how fearful I was of Piper being bitten by him. While she was putting on a brave face, her insides were in turmoil. She didn't want to do this, not in the slightest, but she was pushing back her fear to save Wynn. Piper was doing whatever it took to get the information we needed, just as she proved back at the house with Darren. I'd have been proud of her had I not wanted to scoop her up and run as fast as I could away from here before Morpheus could sink his fangs into her.

"Why, Antoine, what do you think I am? A novice? I haven't killed someone by accident in centuries." Morpheus placed a hand on his chest in mock offense.

"Precisely." I narrowed my eyes on him, lacing my fingers together in front of me on the table. "Now, Wynn?"

Sighing as if he really didn't want to give up the information, but the temptation of Piper's blood was too much for him to hold it back, he confessed, "They're in Nice."

"France?" I arched a brow. "Seems Boris has gone to great lengths to separate us."

"It would seem so, but they won't be there for long," Morpheus continued, his eyes

an acid bath when this was all over or I'd never feel clean again.

His hands lifted until they came to the tie on my halter top. I hitched a breath and one of the guys stepped toward me. Morpheus simply smiled down at me. "We wouldn't want to get blood all over that pretty top of yours."

I waved whoever had stepped forward off, allowing Morpheus to untie my shirt. I held the front up against my breasts. He might be getting to drink my blood, but that didn't give him the right to the rest of my body.

Morpheus spun me around, making me face the others. "It's so much better with an audience, don't you think?" His sharp nail stroked the side of my neck, not cutting, but the threat of violence was there.

My eyes drifted over to Rayne's of their own accord. The muscles in his jaw were tight, his body poised to launch forward at any moment. *Please don't.* I shoved the thought at him, hoping to calm him some. I might not be able to make myself chill out, but I couldn't have the others getting hurt for this. It was my decision. It had to be me.

Morpheus combed my hair away from my neck, his nose inhaling my scent. "Magnificent. I can see why they're so taken with you."

"Morpheus." Antoine's warning tone held more violence in it than I'd ever heard. "Stop torturing her. Get your taste before my brothers can no longer wait."

Huffing, Morpheus practically sounded like a chastised child, whining, "You take all the fun out of it. I'm regretting giving you the information."

"Be that as it may, you did. Now finish this." Antoine warned once more, his gaze locked on to the vampire behind me.

Morpheus didn't even give me any warning before he struck. His fangs sank so deeply into my neck, I swore he was scratching bone. Tears filled my eyes and I held back a scream by biting my lip. I wouldn't give him the satisfaction.

While Morpheus's bite hurt like a son of a bitch, it wasn't the same as Valentine's. His had been brutal like a vicious animal. Add in the fact that he was trying to kill me and I couldn't call out to any of the guys, it was a human's worst nightmare. Morpheus was child's play after that.

Pain radiated from my neck and throughout my body, causing it to stiffen up. I couldn't move away from him no matter how much I wanted to. His grip on my head ached, my neck overextended for far too long. His other arm wrapped around my waist, pulling me back against his chest so I could feel the hard-on in his pants. It made me sick to my stomach.

"Enough," Antoine announced, his tone clipped, leaving no room for argument.

All at once, Morpheus released me with a moan. "Oh, yes. That's the stuff." His hands went to my shoulders, massaging them as he whispered in my ear. "I'll be dreaming of you tonight, dear. Thank you for that."

I shuddered in revulsion and forced my feet forward, anything to get away from him, but I only made it two steps before my knees wobbled and gave out. Marcus was there to catch me, even though he was the farthest away. I held my shirt with one hand and clutched Marcus's shirt with the other, breathing him in.

"Let's get out of this shit hole," Drake growled, and we all moved out.

If any of them were threatening Morpheus, I wouldn't know. I was trying not to think of anything right now. If I did, then I might start screaming and I wasn't sure I'd ever be able to stop.

The club was silent, the beating drum of the music no longer playing around us. Even in my numb state, I could feel the tension in the room. Someone moved closer to us and

Marcus stiffened his arms around me, a low grumble coming from his chest.

"I smell blood," an unknown vampire hissed, but then in the next heartbeat he yelped before his body hit the floor with a loud thud.

"Anyone else?" Drake snarled, his voice saying he was more than ready for a fight, would enjoy it even. Unfortunately for him, no one took him up on his offer, and we made it through the club and down the long, winding hallway. Nobody stopped us as we went through the metal door, and before I knew it, I was back inside the limo.

Marcus gently placed me down in the backseat, taking the seat opposite me. All but Darren piled in after us, who I assumed sat in front with the driver. Antoine settled next to me this time, with Rayne on the other side, while the twins sat with Marcus, their eyes tight and their mouths pressed into thin lines. The twins' gaze kept drifting to my neck where I was still bleeding.

"Here," Rayne placed a cloth from the limo's mini bar against my neck.

I winced at the stinging that came from the contact. I let my eyes flutter closed and held the cloth against my neck, leaning into Rayne's embrace. The car lurched forward and we were moving. I wasn't sure where we were going, but as long as it was far away from Morpheus and Club Dead, I didn't care.

After a few moments, something moved in front of my face and I peeked my eyes open to see Antoine's bleeding wrist in front of me, the sharp tinge of his blood overriding the scent of my own.

"Drink," he commanded, his expression neutral except for a slight tightness around his lips.

Anger pushed through the pain and I shoved his arm away. "No, keep your blood. I don't want to be bound to you any more than I already am right now. I'd like my own thoughts and feelings if you don't mind."

Antoine sighed, rubbing his forehead with one hand. "This is not the time to be difficult, Piper. I warned you—"

"I know," I clipped, picking up my bag from the bottom of the limo where I'd left it. "I'm not mad at you. You prepared me as much as you could, but I can't take your blood." My eyes went over the others in the back of the limo. "Any of yours. I need to feel my own feelings without any of you getting the backlash of it. Give me that luxury."

Antoine seemed to want to argue, but he inclined his head. "Very well, but you're going to need stitches." He shifted in his seat so he was facing me, his hand tipping my head to the side to see the damage.

"The fucker did it on purpose," Allister snarled, his arms crossed over his chest as if keeping himself from doing something stupid. Like going back into the club and ripping Morpheus apart. There was something about how protective they were over me that made me feel better. Like the pain was worth it. For this. For them.

I placed my hand on top of Antoine's, squeezing it as I lowered it from my neck. "It's fine."

Rayne's breath touched my shoulder as he said, "But you need medical attention, not only from the blood loss, but he could have given you a bone fracture."

I unzipped my bag and searched around for a moment before finding the vial I had the forethought to bring with me. I held the little vial up so they could see.

"Whose blood is that?" Marcus inquired, suspicion narrowing his eyes. I thought it might have been the longest sentence he'd ever said to me.

I popped the cork and all five vampires inhaled the scent. Understanding seemed to settle in them as I downed the little vial of Wynn's blood.

"When did you get that?" Rayne asked, busying himself with finding water to wash off the blood of the already healing bite mark.

I shot him a look, smirking. "When you broke my hand. Wynn thought I might need some for later. Just in case."

The others glared at Rayne, who held his hands up in his defense. "It was on accident. Geez. Don't stake me."

"Well, it was good of you to think to bring it." Allister dropped his arms and relaxed in his seat. "It'll at least keep us from worrying about you dying on us."

Drake snorted. "More like one of us biting you too." He shifted in his seat, adjusting the front of his jeans not so subtly. "I don't know if you know this, but your blood..." He shook his head and laughed. "It's far too tempting. Even just to smell it."

My mouth dropped open slightly in surprise. My face flushing, I busied myself with retying my shirt and stuttered out, "Uh...thank you? I think."

"Now that Piper is healed, we have other pressing matters to discuss." Antoine laid an arm on the back of the seat, pressing against my shoulders. I let him. Not only because I needed the extra touch myself, but because I had a feeling he did too. Things in

Morpheus's club had been bad, but it could have been worse. A lot worse.

I shoved down the dark thoughts and tuned back in to the conversation. "Where are we going to go now? To France? And what about these hunters? What are they?"

"Vampire hunters," Rayne explained, his face tight with worry. "They hunt our kind for some religious oath or duty."

My lips tugged down in a frown. The only vampire hunters I'd heard about were from movies and books. I'd never thought they would be real too. Then again, a short while ago I didn't believe in vampires. So, as far as I knew, there could be a whole slew of supernaturals I didn't know about.

"What makes them so special? How can they even go up against you guys?" I glanced around the limo, not seeing how a bunch of religious zealots could even make a dent in them.

"Somewhere down the line, they made a deal with some witches so they aren't any more human than we are," Allister elucidated with a scoff. "They can scent us, and if they see you then they can find you. No matter where you go."

"Which is why it is imperative that we keep a low profile," Antoine added, giving me a sideways look. "They never back down from a hunt. Ever." I swallowed thickly and nodded. So, we don't want to be caught by the hunters. Got it. That only made finding Wynn even more urgent before these hunters got a whiff of him.

Oblivious to my thoughts, Antoine continued to my next question. "Going to France is the logical next step." He placed his hand on his chin, tapping his lips with one finger. "Unfortunately, Morpheus had been right on time. Even with our own plane we don't have time to go home and pack and get to Nice before Boris takes off with Wynn."

"So, we go to Frankfurt?" Rayne surmised, placing his hand in my lap. I curled my fingers around it, giving him a small smile.

Antoine sighed, and for the first time ever, I saw an uncertainty in his expression. "If that is indeed where they are going. Our master—Boris—might be a murderous bastard, but he's only lasted this long because he is also clever."

The others nodded in agreement. Drake pulled out his phone and tapped a few things out. "I'll check with my contacts in Nice and see if they've left yet. Not that they had known they were there in the first place," he muttered under his breath, and then glanced over at his twin. "Allister, check with Mari, she still lives in Frankfurt, right?"

Allister took his own phone out and flipped through a few pages, typing something as well. "As far as I know. I'll see if anyone has been told to prepare for their arrival."

"Good." Antoine nodded, a bit more sure of himself but not quite. "Good. And we'll..." He paused for a long moment, and then to my surprise, he turned to me. "You should rest. You've lost a lot of blood. I don't want you to faint on us at a crucial moment." He brushed my hair away from my face, his thumb trailing down my cheek to trace my lower lip. "I do wish things had ended differently."

My brows furrowed at his words, not understanding what he meant. If he was talking about with Morpheus, then I agreed with him completely. I didn't want another vampire's fangs in me that didn't belong there. My body warmed at the thought of the last vampire with their teeth in me who I had actually wanted to bite me. A collective groan in the limo made my face heat and I ducked my gaze, muttering an apology.

"Can we get out of here already?" Drake grunted, and I peeked up to see his heated gaze on me. "All this blood and arousal is going to drive me crazy."

"Yes," Antoine agreed, taking my chin in his hands. "I do this for your own good and the sanity of the rest of us. You can yell at me later."

I frowned at him, about to ask what he meant, when his power swept over me as he commanded, "Sleep." Then all I knew was blissful nothingness.

Chapter 12
Marcus

THE DRIVE TO OUR hangar was tense and mostly silent. While Piper slept in Rayne's arms, none of us were in the mood to talk. Besides, we would have a whole plane ride to figure out what we were going to do next.

Going to France was the best choice, since we knew Wynn was already there. Even if we missed him, then we might find some kind of clue on where to find him. I agreed with the others on the Frankfurt point. It was too obvious of a choice and Boris was far too smart to let where he was going get around unless he wanted it to. If the hunters were on their trail, then it was probably a decoy to throw them off the scent.

I picked up Piper and lifted her out of the limo. Something about Piper had changed inside me. Where I'd thought she was a hindrance before, and I still wasn't sure she wasn't, the way she stepped up to Morpheus, not letting Rayne take more pain into himself than he already had, had been a selfless act that I never thought the human had in her. From what I'd seen of the human maid turned human servant, she was clumsy, too talkative for her own good, and didn't know when to quit. The last part I could understand. I'd never been the type to give up and Piper seemed to be the same.

I stared down at the woman in my arms as she sighed and shifted closer to me. Even in her sleep she wanted to be near me. It was like she had been made for us, drawn to each of us for different reasons, and though those reasons weren't clear, I was finding the guards surrounding my heart dropping around her.

The others were working on getting the plane ready for takeoff. Darren had been on the phone since we got here, talking to different people about things we needed. Since we didn't have time to pack, there were provisions we required. Blood. Clothes. Human food. While the plane had some things, there wasn't enough for all of us for the long trip—if we made it to where we were going.

Walking up the stairs, I pushed past the curtains, not acknowledging the staff who were staring at me. They must be new. Our usual staff knew better than to stare and to keep their arousal in check. Two of the females flared up with want as I passed them, and even more so when Drake and Allister came in right behind me. My lip curled up into a sneer.

Other humans' arousal I couldn't handle. They stunk like burning garbage, stinging the nose and making my stomach roll.

Another person's arousal hit my nose, but this one came from the woman in my arms. Piper buried her face into my chest, shifting her thighs against one another. Unlike the others, her arousal did things to me. My shaft hardened against my pants, my fangs ached to be inside her, and I had to push back the need just to take another step forward. Shoving down my desire to plunge into her in more ways than one, I strode across the cabin to the bedroom in the back.

Laying her down on the bed, I withdrew my arms, but Piper's hand wouldn't let go of my shirt. She moaned in her sleep, pulling me closer to her. I braced myself on the bed around her, my hold on my need lessening the longer she kept me there. It didn't help that she still wore the outfit from the club. The fishnet stockings and mini skirt did nothing to minimize her scent.

Piper's legs spread, her skirt pushing farther up her legs, exposing the femoral artery in her inner thigh. My eyes zeroed in on it, her blood pumping through the vein, making it pulsate. I found myself leaning into her, my fangs extended and an unreasonable hunger pushed at my self-restraint.

"Marcus." Antoine's voice snapped me out of whatever trance I had been in.

I jerked away from Piper, ripping my shirt from her hand in the process. She groaned in protest, but rolled over and went back to sleep. Stepping away from her, I walked out of the room. "Are we ready?"

"Almost." Antoine peered down at Piper's sleeping form, his lips pursed in concentration. Turning from the door, he shut it quietly behind him. "We're headed to Nice," Antoine began, not even questioning what I'd been doing with Piper. Perhaps because he trusted me, or maybe he just didn't care if she was with me. She was already with Rayne and Wynn as well, what was one more?

I inclined my head. We took our seats in the cabin, the others already having taken theirs. The twins, who would usually be breaking out a pack of cards by now, were pensive, their gazes focused at the floor. Rayne had his phone out, playing some game that made annoying beeping sounds. He wasn't acting much different, but the mind reader had the worst gift of us all. I didn't blame him for wanting to keep his focus on other things. I couldn't imagine having to listen to other's thoughts, having to deal with your own was bad enough.

Antoine sat back in his chair and crossed one leg over the other. "Since we don't have any clue if our master will be heading to Frankfurt or somewhere else, the only probable place to start is where they were last." Darren appeared in the doorway with a tray in his hand loaded with glasses. Antoine reached up and picked up the tumbler of scotch from Darren. No wine this time. Seemed even Antoine was feeling the pressure.

Drake snorted. "Like he would be stupid enough to leave anything behind." He shook his head, almost knocking Darren over when he held his tray out to him. Drake downed his drink in one gulp, gripping the glass tumbler in his hands tightly. "We should just admit it. We don't know our heads from our asses. We'll need a miracle to find Wynn. Let alone with the hunters sniffing around."

"Are you saying we should just give up?" Allister sneered at his brother in disbelief, taking his drink from Darren with a grateful smile. He didn't drink the dark liquid in his glass, only holding it in his hands, his expression turning dark. "We can't do that."

"That's not what Drake is saying at all." Rayne glanced up from his phone, waving Darren off when he offered him a drink.

"Stay out of my head, dickwad," Drake snarled at Rayne, baring his fangs at him. "I can speak for myself."

"Stop projecting so loudly and I would," Rayne snapped, his hands gripping both sides of his chair.

"Now, now, we cannot turn on each other in this time of crisis." Antoine slid his fingers through his hair, his gaze hard with annoyance. "Wynn has very little time, and we need to figure out a plan before we end up on the other end of the hunter's stake."

"He started it," Rayne grumbled, pushing back into his seat as he crossed his arms over his chest and pouted.

Such a child.

Rayne shot me a glare, but I ignored him. If he didn't want to hear what people thought of him, he shouldn't be listening.

"Those damn hunters." The glass in Drake's hand cracked before shattering. He let the pieces drop to the ground with a grunt. Darren was there moments later, picking up the shards with careful precision. Drake didn't even glance down at Darren, his anger consuming him. "What I wouldn't give to have five minutes alone with one of those fuckers."

"You'll give your life, that's what." Allister smacked his brother on the arm, earning him a glower. "Don't be so rash. We have lived this long by avoiding the hunters. We can't let up now just because we're desperate to get Wynn back. We don't want to lose anyone else."

Drake's expression dropped as he sagged back into his seat. "Still, I hate this feeling of helplessness. I hate that we can't do anything to help Wynn. Who knows what that monster is making him do right now?"

"Wynn will be alright," Antoine reassured him, handing his glass to Darren as he passed by. "He knows how to be careful without giving the master too much."

"It's not our master that I'm worried about," Drake grumbled, rubbing his hands over his face. "With Wynn's powers, you know Boris will make him use them on whoever he wants to gain an advantage over.

And I think we all remember what that entails." His gaze drifted over to the bedroom door where Piper's soft breathing could be heard coming from the other room. "I don't know if Piper will be able to handle what Wynn will have to do to survive."

"I wouldn't be so sure about that." Rayne leaned forward in his chair, his elbows propped up on his knees as he rested his face on his hands. "Piper has already proven she would do what it took to get Wynn back. She even put herself into an uncomfortable position even though she had been recently attacked by Valentine. All to get information on Wynn and keep me from being made the victim." Rayne stared down at the floor hard, his mind elsewhere even as he spoke. "If you think that whatever Wynn has to do would make Piper not want to be with him, then you don't know her as well as you think."

Drake quieted after that. His own thoughts swirling behind his eyes. Allister as well, though he kept looking to the bedroom door. It made me wonder what else I had missed while I collected information.

It was Antoine who broke the silence. "There's no use worrying about what will happen once we get Wynn back. We have to save him first. Then we can deal with whatever consequences that come."

"Agreed." I crossed my arms over my chest, nodding. Darren came back out of the refreshments area once more, this time with only one glass. Blood.

He walked it over, not offering it directly to me, but setting it on the table in front of me. One thing I could say for the man was he adjusted well to anticipating our needs. I didn't take things from anyone, especially humans. One too many backstabbers. I'd learned early that humans couldn't be trusted when a horde of them tried to take me out. My arms tightened until my muscles tensed with the strain.

All humans were the same. Conniving and power hungry. They did whatever it took to get what they wanted. The only exception I'd seen so far was Darren, who only did what he thought would make our lives easier. Though, in a way, I supposed it was for self-gain as well. The longer Antoine lived, the longer he would. Although, I wasn't sure that was why he did it.

Piper, however, I didn't know what her motivation was. She didn't become a human servant to live longer or to save her own life. She did it because we told her it was the only way to keep Valentine away from her. Then, there was the way she had taken up for Rayne back at Morpheus's. What did she gain from letting herself be the victim over Rayne? It wasn't the first time Rayne had to endure such hardships in the name of our family. Most of those were at the hands of Boris, but still, he'd get over it eventually after a few weeks of sulking. She didn't need to put herself in danger.

So, why?

For love?

The very idea of her actions being motivated by love for one of my brothers was absurd to me. Humans and vampires couldn't be together. It never worked out. Even when they were human servants. The humans always wanted more. Either to be changed into a vampire or they wanted children, a family of their own. Something they couldn't get from a vampire.

I sat back in my chair, my eyes drifting once more to the bedroom door. *What is it about you, Piper Billings? Why do you make my head feel so scrambled?* I mused.

Chapter 13
Piper

THE SOFT GRASS BENEATH me caressed my bare skin and feet. The sun beat down on my skin, warming my body and keeping back the chill of the breeze blowing through the hill I laid on. As far as dreams went, this one beat the others a hundred to one.

I didn't know where my subconscious pulled this place from. It certainly wasn't from anywhere I'd ever been. The rolling hills stretched out as far as the eye could see. An abnormal silence filled the area. Usually, even without cars and people, there was some kind of sound. Birds chirping, bugs making whatever sounds bugs made, something. Anything.

Unfortunately, the silence wasn't the only weird thing about this dream. If I'd been in control, I'd be laying out on the grass in a pretty sundress and maybe one of those floppy hats. What I wouldn't be doing is laying here in a tiny white string bikini when there was no water in sight.

"I had a dream like this once," a familiar voice commented, and I lifted my head as Wynn lounged next to me on the grass. "Except you were naked, and we weren't at my childhood home."

My brows furrowed at him. "So, this is your dream?"

"No." Wynn shook his head, his dark hair falling into his face before he sighed. "And yes."

Now I was confused.

With no immediate, looming danger, I settled back onto the grass with Wynn by my side. "So, are you in my head or am I in yours?" I muttered more to myself than to Wynn.

"Both. Neither." Wynn turned his head, his pretty blue eyes sparkling with mischief as I shifted to meet his gaze.

I smiled and curled onto my side to watch him. "Now you're purposely being evasive."

"Perhaps." Wynn shifted onto his side as well, his hand reaching out to thread his fingers through my hair. "Perhaps I am just trying to delay. I want to make this last while I can."

My lips tugged down into a frown. What was he talking about? Wynn cupped my cheek, causing my doubts to flitter away as I leaned into his touch. "I missed you." My voice came out small and quiet.

"And I you, lovely Piper." Wynn's gaze grew soft as he scanned my face, almost memorizing it. For what reason, I didn't know. I wasn't going anywhere.

We sat there quietly for a few moments, just basking in each other's presence. Nothing good can last that long though. Something always had to mess it up.

"You drank my blood." Wynn paused his stroking of my face, his expression growing serious. "What happened?"

I tipped my head to the side, not sure what he was talking about. Then I sat up, remembering what had occurred before I came here. My hand went to my neck where Morpheus had bitten me. The bite was gone and there wasn't any bleeding, but it was a dream, that didn't mean anything in real life.

"I got hurt," I murmured, slowly dropping my hand from my neck. "We were trying to find you and..." My voice cracked, my eyes burning with tears. "I'm sorry you were taken for me."

"Shh, shh, precious. It's going to be alright. Come here." Wynn sat up, wrapping his arms around me until I was in his lap. It seemed Wynn's desire for me to be in a bathing suit only went so far, because he wore his normal clothing—black slacks and a white, billowing, button-down shirt. What a sight we must have made.

I pressed my face to his neck, not caring that I was getting him all wet with my tears. "If it wasn't for me then you would be here. It's all my fault."

"No, it's not." Wynn smoothed his hand up and down my back in a soothing manner. "It's Boris's. He only used you to do what he's been trying to do for several centuries. Get us back under his thumb."

"Still..." I sighed into his embrace. "If it weren't for me..."

"Hey now." Wynn pulled me back, his eyes locking with mine in a serious stare. "I have no regrets. I would do it again a thousand times just to keep you safe, and I'm sure the others would have done the same."

I wiped at my face and shook my head. "Not all of them." I gripped the front of his shirt. "I did such terrible things to just get information about where you were. I..." My voice caught in my throat as I tried to tell him what happened. Unable to say what I did, I dropped my chin to my chest. "Can you forgive me?"

"Oh, pet." Wynn tipped my chin up, brushing his lips against mine. "There is nothing to forgive. Whatever you had to do, I know you did it for me, just as I have had to." I nodded, still uncertain how he would feel about me having sex with Darren or letting Morpheus bite me. But he was right, we were both doing what we must to survive and get him back.

Sniffing once more, I looked away from the intensity of his stare, unable to bear it. "So, this is where you grew up?"

Wynn frowned but didn't question my change in topic. "Not really. I was actually born over there." He pointed at a hill off to the west. "Just over that hill stood my family's farm. I lived there until my father passed away. Then we lost the farm and had to make our own way in the world."

Saddened by his story, I slid my hands up his chest and stroked my thumb along the line of his jaw. "How old were you?"

His eyes dipped down to mine. "Not much younger than you actually. Now, no more talk of sad stories or mistakes we have made." Wynn's hands slid down my back, grabbing a handful of my ass. "By my estimate, we have a few hours before one of us gets interrupted."

A coy smile crept up my face, my arms going around his neck as I pressed myself closer to him. "Oh, what ever could we do?"

Wynn cocked a brow and smirked. "I have a few ideas."

My mouth descended on his, digging my hands into his hair. We weren't close enough. A part of me had been missing since he was taken, and I didn't want to ever be away from him again.

Grinding my hips down on his lap, I smiled against his lips with satisfaction as he groaned, his hands tightening on my ass. Wynn never released me from the toe-curling kiss, while his fingers worked on the ties of my bikini. As the material dropped away, Wynn pulled back from the kiss, his eyes devouring every inch of me. "I am so happy you drank my blood. Maybe we should make it a habit for you?"

I giggled. When he cupped my breasts, tweaking my nipples, my laugh turned into a moan. "Mmm. Put it in my morning coffee perhaps?"

Wynn hummed, his mouth dropping to the tops of my breasts. "Sounds like a plan to me."

"Except—" I gasped at the feel of his fangs pressing against my flesh, not breaking the skin, as he took a peak into his mouth. "We have opposite schedules. We'd never be asleep at the same time."

"I'm not asleep now," Wynn explained, and then without warning, the bottoms of my bathing suit were gone, leaving me bare to his hungry gaze.

Wanting to keep going but unable to just leave it alone, I pulled at his shirt until it was off his shoulders and asked, "Then how are you here?"

"I'm on a plane." Wynn grunted as my hand dove into the front of his pants, not patient enough to wait to get them off. "I simply felt you in the back of my mind and knew. As far as anyone else knows, I'm pouting about being forced to move again, when really—" He hissed as I pulled him out of his pants and rubbed the head of him against my folds. "I'm here with you."

"Yes." I beamed before sinking down on him with a gasp. "You are here with me."

The sounds coming from my mouth would have embarrassed me in real life, but for some reason the knowledge that I was dreaming helped me let go. There was no one here but us, and I was going to make the most of it.

I rode Wynn, my chest rubbing against his, causing small bursts of pleasure to rocket through me. Wynn's mouth pressed kisses against every part he could reach—my cheeks, my nose, my lips, even the tips of my ears—before settling on my neck where Morpheus had recently bit me.

"No!" My eyes flipped open and I pulled back from him but didn't move off of his length. "Don't. I can't. Not so soon after..." I trailed off, unable to tell him what happened. The memory flashed through my mind and I felt the world around us waver. The trees disappeared, the walls of Morpheus's office appearing in their place. "No, no!" I cried out, and not just from pleasure. It was like a really fucked up sex dream. While Wynn drove me toward orgasm, the world around me morphed into one of the worst things that had happened to me. The grass beneath us transformed into ugly brown carpet. The small table Antoine and Morpheus had sat at appeared next, right next to my face.

"Piper, what's happening?" Wynn tried to draw me back to him. "You have to focus on me. Don't think about it. If you don't, I can't stay here, I'll be thrown out." Wynn's concern only added to my own panic, my heart pounding like a drum in my chest. Or dream,

I didn't know the logistics, I just knew I was freaking out.

I shook my head, tears streaming down my face. "I can't make it stop. Wynn, please." I clung to him, trying to keep him here and wishing the image to go away. "Please, Wynn, make it go away. Don't leave me."

Wynn rubbed up and down my back, no longer moving his hips against mine. "I can't. It's your mind that's changing it. You have to fix it." Wynn lifted my face to his, a serious note to his voice. "Take it back, Piper. Make this memory yours."

My brows furrowed in confusion. "I... I can't. This is my memory. How can I change it?"

His lips ticked up at the sides. "Yes, you can." Pushing up onto his knees, his length still hard and deep inside of me, making me moan, he lifted us. My legs went around his waist as I held on. Sitting me down on the table, he took my face in his hands. "What happened next? What happened in this room?"

I closed my eyes and shook my head, unable to bring myself to say it. Without me knowing it, or trying to make it happen, a presence appeared near us. I squeaked, my eyes flying open as I expected Morpheus to be there, right in front of me. But it was

Antoine, sitting there with an annoyed, impatient expression on his face, and a glass of wine in his hands. "We went to Club Dead. To see Morpheus." Wynn stiffened against me, pushing in deeper, making us both groan. As if speaking about him made him real, Morpheus sat in the opposite chair from Antoine, his pet human sitting at his feet a few inches away from us.

"Why would you go to see that manipulative child abuser?" Wynn growled out, his face more angry than turned on now.

My nails dug into his biceps and I tried to recall what happened. "He knew information on where you'd gone, but he wouldn't give it to us for free."

"Of course not." Wynn tangled his hand in my hair, the other one gripping my hip. "Morpheus never does anything that doesn't benefit him. What did he want?"

I dropped my gaze to where we were connected still, trying to push the feeling of panic away from my chest. When I felt like I could breathe again, I lifted my gaze to his once more. "Me. Always it's me. Why? I'm nothing special. Why do I always get everyone else in danger?" My throat thickened with emotion. "What's wrong with me?"

Wynn shook his head vehemently. "Nothing. And none of this is your fault." When I calmed down enough to continue, Wynn drew my attention once more. "We don't have much time left. What happened next? I can't hold on to the dream much longer."

Licking my lips, I struggled to get the next words out. "Morpheus attacked us in the club, but we got away and came rushing into here to save Antoine." Seconds later, the group of us rushed into the room, clad in our club attire.

Wynn's gaze slid over to where I stood, his lips quirking up. "Nice outfit."

I smacked his chest with a weak laugh. "Stop it. It's all I had on short notice." As I watched the silent exchange between Morpheus and the rest of us, my laughter died. "Morpheus wanted me for the information. When Antoine denied him, he tried to take Rayne. I wouldn't let him."

My memory self walked forward, pushing Rayne back. Looking at myself now, I saw the determination on my face as well as the fear. It was then I realized, I would do it again. Even though it hurt. Even though it scared me to my bones, I'd do it again to save Rayne the pain, to see the look of relief on his face that I couldn't see before but could see now.

"Just a taste, he'd said," I murmured, chuckling bitterly.

Wynn groaned. "Don't laugh, please. I can't stay still much longer." To prove his point, his hips thrust forward, and I swallowed my next words. "What happened next?"

I forced myself to focus on my memory self. "He bit me. In front of everyone, and for some reason, it was almost worse than when Valentine bit me. Not because I knew he wouldn't kill me, but because I couldn't cry out without causing them pain. They were right there, and I had to just take it."

"No." Wynn pulled back and grabbed my hand, pushing me toward the memory of me and Morpheus. We moved through them as if they were ghosts. Wynn took Morpheus's place and maneuvered me in front of him, his arm sliding around my naked waist. Brushing my hair to the side, his mouth touched my ear. "We can make this memory yours. It won't haunt you anymore. Are you willing to try?"

My breathing quickened and my hands were sweaty, if they could be in a dream. I leaned back into his embrace, forcing myself to take slow breaths, and tilted my head to the side. "I'll try."

"That's my girl."

I braced myself, thinking Wynn was going to bite me, but his mouth didn't even come near my neck. His tongue slid along the edge of my ear and then he pulled it into his mouth, sucking on it. It caused my insides to clench deliciously and my thighs rubbed together. A distant part of me wondered if I was making these sounds in my sleep and if the others could hear me. Except right now, I wasn't going to be embarrassed. I'd worry about it later.

Wynn's hand slid down my stomach and dipped between my thighs while his other cupped my breast. My breathing picked up now, but not from fear, from desire. His fingers moved in slow, practiced movements around my clit, and I found myself thrusting into his hand, my back arching into his touch. I barely noticed the fact that his mouth had drifted to my neck, placing hot, open-mouthed kisses along the place Morpheus had bitten me.

The thickness of Wynn's cock pressed against my backside and I rubbed against it. Wanting him back inside me just as much as I wanted his fingers on me. The sharp sting of his fangs trailed over my neck, and instead of being afraid, I could feel myself getting even more turned on. My head tilted to the side on its own, and a small whimpering sound came from my throat. "Please."

"Please what?" Wynn breathed against my neck. "What do you want, Piper?"

Rocking against his hand, I reached up and gripped the back of his head, urging him forward. "Bite me."

I cried out as my release hit me at the same moment his fangs pierced my skin. I clung to his head, my hips jerking as my knees quaked beneath me. Wynn held me to him, keeping me from falling to the ground. Unlike Morpheus's bite, Wynn pumped pheromones into me, making me come again just from his bite. I moaned and sagged against him like a junkie finally getting their fix after a long dry period.

After what felt like forever, Wynn released my neck and slowly lowered us to the soft grass. My eyes were hooded as I took in the rolling hills once more. "I did it," I breathed, slightly high on the whole experience.

"Yes, you did." Wynn laid down next to me, pressing his body against mine but not trying for anything more. "I'm so proud of you."

I smiled softly, feeling like I might sink into the ground at any moment. After a minute, I lifted my gaze to his. "Hey, how do your powers work if I'm dreaming? That's a little crazy, even for vampires."

A hint of a grin quirked Wynn's lips. "My blood inside you gives me the connection. I can use my powers on you from anywhere because of it."

I smirked. "Kinky."

"Yes," Wynn agreed with a chuckle, his hand sliding up and down my side. "It can be."

I hummed and settled into his embrace once more. Then something came to me, something I had been so stupidly distracted to not think of before. "Wait a minute. You're here."

"Yes, love. We established this already." His eyes laughed at me as I sat up and shook my   head.

"No, I mean you can tell me where you are." I patted his arm, excitement surging through me.

"What do you mean? I thought Morpheus told you."

I frowned hard. "Only that you were in France and headed to Frankfurt, but the others think that's a lie."

Wynn inclined his head. "We were in France, yes, but have since left. I mentioned before I was on a plane." His eyes traveled down the length of my naked body. "You were otherwise distracted."

"So, you are going to Frankfurt?" I kept going, not letting myself get distracted again.

Wynn pursed his lips. "No. Boris mentioned it once, but even though he never said where exactly we are going, I figured it out well enough. He could not hide the familiar mountain ranges and cities of his home country. Even he is not that good." Wynn paused, his expression pinching together. "Someone is trying to wake me."

"Where's his home country?" I prodded, panic setting in. I was so close to finding him. He couldn't go now. "Wynn," I reached for him, but my hand passed through his form. "Wynn! Where are you?" I sprang up in the bed of the airplane, yelling his name, but it was too late, the dream was gone.

The door to the small bedroom was thrown open, revealing Rayne's and Antoine's concerned expressions. Rayne rushed to my side, taking me into his arms, trying to soothe me. "It's alright, Piper. It was just a dream."

I pushed him away, causing him to frown. "No, you're right, it was a dream. A dream of Wynn." I stared at him and then Antoine when they didn't seem to get it. "I took Wynn's blood. So now I dreamed of Wynn." I held my hands out to my sides, frustration coming over me. "For fuck's sake. You're the vampires. You know how your powers work." I took a deep breath as I reiterated, "I drank Wynn's blood. Wynn was in my dream. Ergo..." I stared at them, waiting for them to catch on. "I know where Wynn is."

"You do?" Drake appeared in the doorway, along with Allister, forcing Antoine to step into the bedroom. "Where is he?"

I shook my head, my hands gripping the blankets beneath me. "I don't know for sure. He said they weren't going to Frankfurt." I paused and struggled to recall his exact wording. "Wynn said something about Boris not being able to hide the mountain ranges of his home country, but he got pulled away before he could tell me where." I lifted my gaze to Antoine's. "Please tell me you know where that is."

"Yes, unfortunately, I do." Antoine's mouth pressed into a thin line. "We're going to Bulgaria. The vampire capital of the world."

Chapter 14
Antoine

I HAD NEVER WANTED to come back to Bulgaria. I had hoped never to see it, let alone set foot in the god-awful country ever again.

I spent the majority of the first couple of decades of my life there, surrounded by Boris and his many children. There were more masters like him in that country. Those who seemed more monster than human. Those who would need a calculator just to count the number of years they had been alive—if any of them remembered that much.

Being a vampire meant both being a part of time and being separate from it. The world changed around you, and if you were smart you changed with it. There were some who refused to change. Those were the ones who still hid in dark alleyways preying on the unsuspecting. The ones who didn't believe in mingling with humans no matter the reason. The majority of them never even took a human servant. They had slaves. Walking, breathing blood bags and nothing more. These kinds of vampires were the ones who lived in Bulgaria.

And Boris was taking Wynn there.

I feared for my brother just as I feared for the rest of my family for having to go there to save him. I especially feared for Piper. Darren knew the risks. While he had never gone to Bulgaria, he had heard me speak about it on several occasions and none of those were happy.

If Piper thought the way she had to act at Club Dead was degrading, she didn't want to know what was expected of her in Bulgaria.

The capital of Bulgaria, Sofia, was the heart of the vampire community. One would think our kind would be more subtle than that with them keeping to the old ways, but even ancient vampires had a need for extravagance. They longed to be out in the light, to not have to hide what they were, and many wished to be worshipped as the gods they thought themselves to be.

I had never wanted that kind of life. It disgusted me the way they penned humans like they were cattle waiting to be slaughtered. With the modern world capturing everything on video and health departments checking into any food business, it was much harder for them to hide their human slaughterhouses. Sadly, they still existed. They just moved the humans into even worse conditions and lost more of them than they were able to bleed.

How they could stomach drinking the blood of someone who lived in constant terror or drugged oblivion was beyond me. Blood tasted so much finer and more exquisite when the donor was willing, even more so when it came from a loved one during intercourse.

My gaze drifted over to Piper, where she sat in her seat on the plane. We were set to descend any moment now, and her anxiety hadn't lessened since she woke. She, of course, wasn't talking to me. Which was fine for now. I'd forced her to sleep when she didn't want to, but in doing so we were able to get our first real information about Wynn's whereabouts. I couldn't feel guilty for that. She seemed to be able to hold a grudge in any case.

Thankfully, she was distraught enough that she no longer became aroused at the single drop of a hat. Sitting in here while she slept and dreamed, smelling so intoxicating and whimpering so sweetly, became unbearable for any of us in the cabin. Draconius had even threatened to climb out on the wing if something wasn't done.

Rayne had been on his way to wake her up when Piper had screamed Wynn's name in her sleep. To find out she had been speaking to Wynn had been a relief to say the least. I didn't need to know why she had become so aroused during that time, the lech couldn't keep his hands to himself in the real world. In a dream world, he was probably taking full advantage of what he could do. Though, with the way Piper had been uncharacteristically quiet, I wasn't sure that was all that happened in there.

I had tried to ask, but Piper didn't even give me a chance. She turned on me, choosing to sit between the twins while drinking heavily from the glass of champagne Darren had provided. She even spoke to him more than she would even look at me. Not that making sure she was happy with me was the most important thing right now. Still, with being able to feel her emotions, it was hard to ignore the anger she felt toward me right then.

"She'll forgive you," Marcus grumbled from my side.

My gaze shifted over to the larger vampire and I cocked a brow. "I didn't think you cared one way or the other."

Marcus lifted a shoulder and dropped it. "She's grown on me."

I snorted, my eyes going back to where Piper had laughed at something one of the twins had said. "She does have that tendency."

"What do you think our chances are?" Marcus changed the topic from Piper to the problem at hand. I could always rely on him to see the bigger picture.

I held back a sigh of frustration. "Sofia is massive. Knowing where he will be is a step in the right direction, but we could search for months and never find him. Especially if they are keeping him in one of those nasty human farms."

Letting out a disgusted scoff, Marcus lifted the glass in his hand to his mouth. We had all gotten a round of blood in preparation of what might greet us when we landed. I'd downed mine in moments. The combination of Piper's emotions and arousal still tingeing the air put me on edge.

"I'm surprised the hunters haven't burned all of Bulgaria to the ground." Marcus sat his glass down on the table in front of him.

"Yes," I murmured distractedly. "They aren't exactly subtle. Boris would fit right in."

"And Wynn?"

"Wynn will do what he has to. He always does." I uncrossed and recrossed my legs. "I'm not so worried about him as I am about what his being gone has done to this family."

"Yes." Marcus nodded. "It does seem to have caused a tension within. Not just because of our new maid either." He gave me a knowing look before standing from his seat. Without giving me an explanation, he walked toward the front of the plane. Likely checking on our timing.

My mind drifted as I waited for the plane to descend. We would find a hotel to stay in, something off the vampire grid. No need to let them know we were here so soon. Then we would search for Wynn. We'd have to be discreet, keep a low profile. Which would be impossible to do with us all together.

I despised splitting the group up, but I didn't see any other choice. The biggest problem wasn't breaking up the group, but convincing Piper to sit this one out. She'd already proven she was willing to go the distance when she allowed Darren to fuck her. Something I still had mixed feelings about. I cared for Darren and Piper. However, seeing the two of them together made my insides swirl. I wanted them both. I wanted them together. Except seeing them like that, her eyes on him as he gave her pleasure, it had been almost too much for me to bear. I hadn't been angry. I'd wanted to be there right in the thick of it. So instead, like I always did when I was confused, I lashed out. Choosing to piss them both off so they didn't see how vulnerable I felt.

Of course, right after I got Piper off, I went to Darren and made it up to him. He, I knew, would understand. Piper, however, was a bit more high maintenance and needed immediate placating. Just like now. Except she wouldn't even give me the chance.

"Master Durand." Darren stepped up to my side, placing a hand on my seat arm. "We're about to land. There will be a car waiting at the hangar to take us to the Hotel Grand. I have made arrangements for clothing as well as personal items to be delivered by the time we arrive."

"Very good." I inclined my head. When Darren moved to leave, I caught his wrist.

Darren kept his expression neutral, shifting back to face me. "Yes, master?"

I urged him forward with two fingers. When he leaned down near my face, I lowered my voice until I was sure Piper wouldn't be able to hear me. "I need you to do something for me, Darren."

"Of course, master," Darren agreed, waiting for me to elaborate. "Anything you need."

"When we get to the hotel, I need you to help me convince Piper to stay behind." My eyes slid past Darren to where Piper prepared for landing. "She won't understand why she needs to stay behind, and I cannot have what happened with Morpheus transpire again. I don't think she, or us, could handle it."

Darren's eyes closed briefly as he jerked his head curtly up and down. "Understood. I will ensure Piper stays at the hotel if I have to tie her to the bed."

I arched a brow at him, and for the first time in the years I've been with him, Darren blushed. Amusement pulled at my lips, but I forced them back into a straight line, waving him off. "Thank you, I'll see you on the ground."

Darren made his way back to the front where he took a seat with the flight attendants. The others hadn't come out to help us the entire flight. Darren had most likely said something to them because of how tense and on edge we had been. Plus, with them being new, it was likely they'd do something that would make one of my brothers lose it. We couldn't afford to have any extra issues on this trip. We had enough on our hands as it was.

The plane shook and bumped as it landed on the ground. We glided into the hangar moments later. The second the doors opened, Piper was up and out of her seat. She was off the plane before any of us could stop her or even think about unbuckling our belts. Sighing with annoyance, I was already mentally preparing myself for the argument I was sure would arise when she realized I wasn't going to let her come.

Once we unloaded the plane and piled into the two cars waiting for us, we were on our way to the hotel. I sat in one car, with Darren in the front seat, and Marcus and Rayne on either side of me. For some reason, Piper had decided that the twins were her new best friends. The buildings of Sofia passed the windows, the night lights making the city's crown joy, Alexander Nevsky Cathedral, with its green and gold domes, look as mysterious as it was beautiful.

Glancing away from the window, I draped my arms over my lap, my phone in one hand ready for the others to contact me at a moment's notice. "What did you do now?"

Rayne glanced up from the game he played on his phone for a brief second before dropping it back to the screen. "What makes you think I did anything?"

My lips ticked up in a knowing smile. "Because you're in here and Piper is in the other car." I jerked my head toward the front of the car. Darren angled his head to the side, not doing a good job pretending not to listen.

Rolling his eyes, but not lifting them from the phone, Rayne muttered, "She doesn't want me in her head."

"Come again?" I shot a look at Marcus to be sure I wasn't hearing things.

Rayne huffed and turned his phone over, glaring at me. "You heard me, don't be a jackass. She doesn't want me reading her thoughts. I guess whatever happened with her and Wynn in her dream wasn't completely pleasant." He shook his head, his red hair falling into his face as he slumped back in his seat. "I mean, can you blame her?"

Marcus snorted. "No."

I arched a brow at Marcus's answer before turning back to Rayne. "Not particularly, but that's beside the point. She needs to be with someone who makes her feel safe. Are you saying she doesn't feel that way about you anymore?"

"I could ask the same about you," Rayne quickly shot back.

I clipped my lips closed and turned to the window. "I did what I had to as we all do. She'll get over it. She just needs time."

"Exactly. Time." Rayne tapped his finger on his phone before the telltale sounds of his game began again. "Something we obviously have in spades."

The sarcasm in his tone wasn't unjustified. We did have loads of time on our hands, but Piper didn't. She might still be my human servant and share my immortality, but that didn't make her indestructible. Whether she hated me for it or not, I would do everything in my power to make sure she got through this. That we would all get through this.

Chapter 15
Allister

HOTEL GRAND HAD CHANGED since the last time we had stayed here. Where it used to be a small, two-story inn made of mostly bricks and wood, now it stood high in the sky, the bottom half grey concrete while the top half had windows from floor to ceiling on every level.

When we stepped into the lobby, shining cream colored tiles had replaced the wooden floor. A bellhop, a freckle faced teenager who couldn't have been more than sixteen, greeted us. Darren and him worked on getting the bags we had on us onto a cart while the rest of us moved toward the front desk.

"Wow!" Piper gaped, her hand tightening around my arm. "This place is huge."

For some reason, after Piper told us where Wynn was, she had latched herself onto my brother and me. I wasn't sure exactly why she was so keen on being with us over Antoine and Rayne, who she was already in bed with, but I also wasn't complaining. If she needed us to be her protectors and confidants right now, then that was what we'd be.

"Haven't been to many hotels, I see." I chuckled, patting her hand, enjoying the warmth of her body so close to mine. My brother stood on the other side of Piper, her arm looped through his as well. The expression on his face smug.

"Nothing like this." Piper took in the light brown wood paneled walls and the leather chairs set out for guests to relax in while they waited. Tasteful art pieces covered the walls, and lamps that had to have cost several thousands of dollars sat on every flat surface. Yes. A far cry from the pit it used to be.

"Well, get used to it." Drake beamed down at her, releasing her arm to wrap it around her waist, pulling her closer to his side. "When you live with us, you live in style."

Piper's lips pursed at his words. "Don't you mean work for?"

Drake's smile dipped and he exchanged a look with me.

Sighing, I rubbed a hand over my face before leading Piper over to the elevators where Darren waited. "Come, you haven't seen everything there is to see. I bet the bedrooms are top notch now."

Piper's heart jumped a little in her chest at my words, and I couldn't help the satisfaction that swirled in my belly at her reaction. While she had already been with Rayne, Wynn, and Antoine, my brother and I hadn't had the pleasure of her company by ourselves. I had a gut feeling that if she already liked us now as friends, then it would be easy enough to persuade her over the line into lover. And my brother and I could be extremely persuasive.

Antoine, Rayne, and Marcus took the first elevator up with Darren, the bellhop taking the other one. We waited for it to come back down, not wanting to be smashed together in such a closed space.

"So, not that I'm looking a gift horse in the mouth," I began, while we waited, "but why are you avoiding Rayne and Antoine?"

Piper stiffened next to me, her mouth turned down in a frown. "I don't want to talk about it."

Drake shook his head and chortled. "Well, you don't have to tell me. I know."

"What? How?" Piper shot him a suspicious glare.

Lifting his hands in defense, Drake gave her a placating smile. "Hey, don't come at me for being observant. It's not like it was hard to figure out."

I cocked my head to the side. "Then do enlighten us, brother."

Dropping his hands to place them in front of him, his eyes went to the little numbers above the elevator, watching the light count down. "You're pissed at Antoine because he made you sleep without your permission. Am I right?"

Piper crossed her arms over her chest, her glare no less intense. "Perhaps."

"And while you're not exactly mad at Rayne, the fact that you don't want to talk about what happened in your dream with Wynn is very telling."

We hadn't been able to convince Piper to tell us anything else about her dream other than Wynn was there and he told her where they were going. The more we pushed her, the more defensive she became. So, we'd dropped it and allowed her to change the subject and drink far too much champagne on the rest of the flight.

"It's obvious that you don't want Rayne to poke through your head about what happened." Drake dropped his gaze to Piper, giving her a knowing look.

Piper scratched the back of her ear and pouted, her eyes dipping to the floor. "It's hard to be dating someone who can peek into your mind whenever they want."

I wrapped an arm around her as the elevator doors dinged and opened. "Welcome to the club, we've had to deal with it all our lives."

"And that's a lot of lives," Drake reminded her, walking into the elevator with us.

We stopped inside the little box, mirrors all around the top half with more wood paneling along the bottom. A golden bar ran along the middle of the walls, which Piper leaned against with a depressed sigh.

"Still, there are some things I just don't want to share with him." Her gaze shifted to both of us in the mirrors. "With anyone. We all have our personal demons and I'd rather keep mine to myself right now. At least until we get Wynn back. I can break down later."

I exchanged a look with Drake, who shrugged. Turning back to Piper, I ran a hand up and down her back. "Don't worry about it. We'll be here to keep you safe, and when the others find Wynn, everything will go back to normal."

Drake coughed and made a cutting move with his hand over his neck, glaring at me.

Piper spun around to face me, her eyes narrowed and her hands on her hips. "What do you mean when they find Wynn? I'm not staying here like some weakling while Antoine and the others get to save Wynn."

Drake scoffed, "You are a weakling." When Piper turned her glare onto him, he quickly added, "I mean, compared to us. Compared to other humans, you are unstoppable. Not a weakling. A goddess really." Drake rambled on and then held his hands out, looking to me for help.

Rolling my eyes at my brother's motor mouth, I placed my hands on Piper's shoulders. "What my brother is trying to say is why don't you sit this one out this time? We're going up against an unknown number of vampires, plus the hunters are bound to show up at some point. We would all feel better if you were somewhere safe."

Piper stared at me for a long minute until the elevator door opened. Then she bolted down the emerald green carpet and bellowed, "Antoine! Where are you?"

"Fuck." Drake covered his ears with a wince. "Now, you've done it."

"What?" I lifted my shoulders as we followed after her. "I thought she knew."

Piper shouted down the hallway until Darren opened a door on the left. "Where is he?" she hissed, pushing past Darren and charging into the room.

We chased after her, waving awkwardly at a few guests who had peeked out their doors to see what the commotion was about. Ducking into the room behind her, Darren shut the door and went back into the kitchenette area off to the left. The hotel suite had a sitting area with couches and chairs sat around an entertainment center, with a large, flat screen television sitting inside of the wooden frame. Several doors lined the walls, which I could only assume went into the bedrooms. While I wanted to see what else had changed in the hotel, nothing was more interesting than the showdown that was about to happen in the middle of the living room.

Piper had planted herself in front of Antoine, her hands on her hips and her eyes spitting fire.

"I will not sit here like some invalid while you go and get Wynn." She jerked her hand in the air and snarled.

Antoine stared down at her with a look of boredom. Not taking her bait. "This is not up for discussion." His eyes shifted to Darren, who didn't meet his gaze. "We have put you in enough danger, don't you think?"

That was the wrong thing to say.

Piper crossed her arms over her chest and leaned back, her expression one of pure disgust. "Oh, so now you care if I'm in danger? It didn't seem so when you made me come with you to Boris the troll's evil manor to flaunt me around like your newest piece of ass, but now you care?" Antoine opened his mouth to argue, but Piper was on a roll. "I thought I had proven to you that I can do this. I fucked Darren. We got the information from Morpheus, which we wouldn't have gotten had it not been for me, and now you suddenly think it's too dangerous?" She curled her fingers into a fist and thrust them down to her sides. "No. Fuck you!"

Before anyone could respond, Piper stomped into the nearby bedroom, slamming the door behind her. The tension in the room could have been cut with a knife. Rayne sat near the window, his eyes on the street, but his shoulders were bunched up almost to his ears. Marcus had his arms crossed over his chest as he leaned against the wall, his expression tight and firm. Antoine turned his stormy gaze onto Drake and me.

Drake lifted his hands. "Don't look at me. I didn't spill the beans."

I lifted my shoulders in defense. "How was I supposed to know she hadn't been told?"

Antoine rubbed a finger against his temples and sighed. "Darren hasn't had a chance to speak to Piper yet."

"Oh." I gave Darren a sheepish grimace. "Sorry."

Antoine waved a hand at Darren. "Will you see what you can do to..." He waved his hand toward the bedroom door Piper had disappeared in to. "Deal with that. We have some planning to do before we can get Wynn back."

Darren bowed at the waist before going to the door. He knocked softly and announced, "It's Darren." Piper must have given him the go ahead, because he turned the knob and entered, closing the door behind him.

With Darren soothing Piper, the rest of us turned to Antoine for instructions.

"So, what's the plan, boss?" Drake prompted.

Antoine took a seat on the light green couch, crossing one leg over the other, his hands settling in his lap. "We know Wynn is somewhere here in the city. Marcus has been in contact with some of his allies here. They have confirmed that Boris arrived a day before we did. There are a few places where Boris likes to spend his time, and while Marcus, Rayne, and myself check them out, you two," he pointed a finger between Drake and me, "will keep Piper safe and above all else, here."

"Why us?" Drake asked before I could. "You're the one banging her."

If looks could kill, Drake would be six feet under right now. Antoine stood, crossing the room in an instant. His hand wrapped around Drake's throat, giving him a warning squeeze. "If you ever speak about Piper that way again, I will make sure it is your last. Are we understood?"

Drake balked, trying to jerk his head in agreement.

"Good." Antoine dropped his hand, releasing Drake. "We don't have a lot of time before the hunters catch up with Boris and we need to act fast. While I despise causing Piper any more distress, right now is not the time to put her in further danger in fear of her feelings."

"Wait a moment." Rayne jumped up from the window, his eyes alight with mischief. "You said the hunters would be here soon."

"Yes," Antoine drawled, "with the evolving world around us, the hunters have joined the modern era and have instant communication. I'm sure they are on their way as we speak."

"What if we fight fire with fire?" Rayne mused, a wicked grin sliding up his face. "Can we get a message to the hunters?" His question was pointed at Marcus.

"Yes."

"Then what if we sent a message telling them where Boris will be?" Rayne arched a brow, trying to get us on the same page.

"You mean like an ambush?" I shook a finger at him, catching onto his train of thought. "The hunters go in and cause a scene, then we sneak in and grab Wynn."

"I like it!" Drake clapped his hands with a hoot. "Let's go!"

"Nah ah ah." I clucked my tongue and slapped my hand on Drake's back. "We're on Piper duty, remember?"

Drake frowned. "Oh, right." He hissed in a breath before blowing it out for some reason, not like we needed to breathe. Old habits and all I suppose. "Fine. Then we are gonna need some drinks and something to keep her busy. 'Cause I'm not dealing with a pissed off human while you guys get all the fun."

Marcus snorted.

Antoine simply shook his head, his pale hair falling over his shoulder. "I think we will have more luck saving Wynn than you will getting Piper to have some fun."

I moved over to the nearby entertainment center and opened the cupboards. Just like I remembered, there were game boxes inside. The last time we came there were wooden boxes of dice and cards, but it seemed with the hotel's makeover, they have updated their games as well. I grinned as I pulled out a box I was sure would improve Piper's mood. "Anyone for Twister?"

Chapter 16
Wynn

I LOUNGED BACK AGAINST the red and yellow cushions in one of Boris's clubs. He had them all over the world, but the one in Sofia was by far the most popular among the vampires. A human would be committing suicide coming in here. The only humans around were so drugged up on pheromones, they weren't worried about the room full of vampires or even getting drained.

The techno music, a bit tacky for my tastes, played so loudly that no one could hear the humans who did have enough of their faculties to scream. I wanted to help them, but unfortunately, I wasn't even in a position to help myself.

The dream with Piper helped ease some of my worries, but also only brought up more problems. It was good to know my family was coming for me. Not that I didn't expect them to save me. It was part of what made us family. However, what Piper has had to endure for me wasn't worth it. I didn't want to destroy everything I loved about her because she was trying to get me back.

I knew on some level Piper felt guilty for what happened. That she thought it was her fault I was taken. It wasn't true. She hadn't even been awake when the decision was made. Everything that had happened up until this point was Boris's fault.

My gaze shifted across the dance floor of the club where vampires bumped and ground against one another. No humans were out there, they'd be swarmed upon in moments. Boris chatted with another master vampire, Nicoli, I believed was his name. He ran the city and kept the humans that were stupid enough to live there from finding out about the vampires. If I had the time or ability, I'd work on outing their whole operation, but as it was, I had enough of my own problems to deal with right now. The hunters being one of them.

"No, sign of the bottom feeding zealots yet." Theresa sat down next to me, a fang tipped smile on her lips. Her dress for the night was made of some kind of plastic in neon pink and greens. She really was taking the techno thing too far.

"Good," I murmured, though a part of me hoped they would find us. If not to kill Boris, then to shut down the human slaughterhouses Nicoli had going on. No one deserved to live like that. If you could call it living.

"Oh, come on, Wynn." Theresa slid her palm along my thigh, leaning close so her breast pushed against my side. "Why so grumpy? We're in the vampire capital of the world, you should be living it up, not sulking over here like a child."

I rolled my head to the side, giving her a lazy smile. "And what would you have me do?"

Her glossy, pink painted lips curled into a wicked grin. "Why, I could think of a few things." Her hand inched up my thigh, but it did nothing for me. Even dream Piper did more for me than her.

I caught her hand in a tight grip before she could touch me. "I've told you before. I'm not interested. Not now, not ever."

Theresa pouted. "You didn't act that way back at the manor. As I remember, you were more than happy to play with me to get what you wanted."

"Exactly." I threw her hand back to her and put my arm up onto the pillows, my eyes shifting away from her and back to the dancers. "You have nothing I want now."

"Are you sure about that?" Theresa cooed, not getting the hint. She practically put herself in my lap as she traced her long nails along my exposed chest where my shirt wasn't buttoned. "I could be the best friend you've ever had if you play your cards right."

I resisted the urge to roll my eyes at her. "I do not need a best friend. Let alone one that comes with strings attached." I glared down at her hand, still on my chest. "The only thing I want is to get out of here, and you can't even break away from Boris yourself."

Theresa huffed, dropping her hand back into her lap. "Why would I want to do that? He provides for me. Keeps me safe. Plus, we're vampires, we should be with our own kind being vampires, not playing pretend at being human." She finally moved off my lap and stood. Her rubber knee high boots squeaked as she moved. "You won't be happy with that human. You need to just get over it and start living your undead life the way you should."

I waved her off, dismissing her and her words. I didn't need advice from someone like her. Theresa had been with Boris for only a few hundred years. She had only seen some of the atrocities he had committed, and most of those had been with her help. Theresa wasn't a vampire to be trusted, no matter what she offered in return.

Thankfully, Theresa got the point and stomped away into the crowd of dancers. She soon found herself a partner and dragged the male vampire with the shaven head down for a kiss. He didn't seem to mind, wrapping his arms around her and pulling her against his bare chest.

Pathetic.

I sat there waiting for the appropriate time for me to leave. Boris would get annoyed if I left too soon without making an adequate appearance, and already my patience was running thin. Counting down the minutes until I could leave was the only thing keeping me sane.

Tired of the strobe lights making spots behind my eyes, I closed my lids and leaned back on the pillows. If anyone knew what was good for them, they wouldn't approach me. When a shadow fell over me and the pillows next to me dipped, I knew I wasn't that lucky.

Not opening my eyes, I growled, "If you value your undead life, you will leave now."

A familiar grunt answered me. "Likewise."

My eyes shot open and I jerked up. "Marcus. What are you doing here?"

The larger vampire glanced over at me, his hands clamped in his lap. "What do you think I'm doing? Rescuing your sorry excuse for an ass."

I snorted. "My ass is perfect, thank you very much. But I mean what are you doing here in this club? If our masters saw you—"

"He won't," Marcus interrupted, his dark gaze moving across the room where I'd last seen Boris. "He and the cretin, Nicoli, have retired to the basement." The way he said the word implied so much more than just a dingy old room. It made me wonder if that was where the humans were kept for slaughter. I also wondered how Marcus even knew about it.

Pushing those questions away for another time, I tried to stand, but Marcus placed a hand on my shoulder and pushed me back down. "What? Let's get out of here while we can."

"Not yet." Marcus shook his head. "Just wait."

Anxious to leave, but not wanting to mess up whatever plan my brothers had in place,

I sat down and sulked. "I'm glad you are here."

Marcus let out another signature grunt. "Of course, you are."

"Where are the others?" I asked, just before an explosion shook the building. The vampires froze, then all hell broke loose. In poured hunter after hunter, covered in shiny black armor, their hands equipped with crossbows. They shot them into the crowd, hitting several vampires in the heart. The remaining vampires scattered, screaming and snarling as they tried to escape. Some of them stayed behind and tried their luck against the hunters. Panic began to fill my chest and I shifted to move again, but Marcus held his hand up.

"Not yet. Wait."

"But they're going to kill us." I jerked a hand toward the hunters, my eyes wide with fear. "We're sitting ducks here."

Marcus didn't answer me, his gaze on the chaos before us. Then, when Boris and Nicoli appeared in the doorway on one side of the club, which I assumed led to the basement, all the hunters focused their attention on them.

"Now." Marcus grabbed my arm and pulled me toward the exit. "We have to get back to the hotel before any of them see us."

I stayed close to his side, keeping my head down so none of the hunters saw me. I didn't want to get out from under Boris's thumb just to have hunters on my tail.

The fighting raged on around us as Marcus shoved his way through the club. The vampires didn't seem to care for us much, but the hunters, the ones who weren't going after the master vampires, were coming right at us.

"Kill anyone who sees you," Marcus growled, pulling two long knives from his boots. He handed me one and headed straight for them.

I gripped the knife in my hands, preparing to spill blood. Fangs were nice and all, but using them against a hunter was only asking to be violently ill. The magic that was used on them to make them our equals in strength and speed also corrupted their blood. One taste of a hunter's blood would take a vampire down. Something some of the other vampires here didn't seem to know. There were several vampires down on their knees, throwing their guts up while the hunter they bit sliced their heads off.

As Marcus dodged and weaved the hunters' arrows, his knife swung out, cutting into them before heading on to the next one. I stood back in his wake, depending on him to kill the majority of them. I could hold my own for the most part, but I was more of a lover than a fighter. Killing someone in cold blood had never been my style, even when they were trying to kill me first.

"Wynn, behind you!" a voice shouted out, which didn't belong to Marcus. Ignoring who the voice might belong to for the moment, I spun in time to barely miss the sword aimed for my head. My foot shot out and kicked the hunter in the side, sending him spiraling across the room and into the wall. He slid down it, leaving a bloody trail along the wall. I ducked another hunter's attack, shoving my own knife into his gut.

Free of attackers for now, I turned back to who had warned me. Antoine stood beside Rayne, fighting their own hunters as they made a clear path for us to escape. I started toward them, hope filling my chest.

"Antoine, Rayne. Am I glad to see you." I grinned from ear to ear as I made my way to their sides. A hunter jumped in between us, but before I had the chance to take him out, Marcus shoved his knife into the hunter's back, straight through his head. Glancing up from the dead hunter to Marcus, I jerked my head in his direction. "Thanks."

"Did you kill the hunters who saw you?" Antoine asked, coming to my side and taking my arm. His pale blue eyes scanned over my form, searching for any injuries.

I glanced back behind me to the hunter I'd thrown to see him still down. "I think so. We should get out of here."

"Yes. Let's go before the masters figure out the ruse." Rayne threw his thumb over his shoulder toward the door and we all hustled out of the club.

The alleyway we exited to was empty, save for a few dead vampires bleeding on the brick road. We kept moving until we made it to a black car waiting a few streets over. Once we all piled in, I turned to my brothers. "You did all this?"

Antoine smirked, obviously pleased with himself. "Yes. A few tips to the right ears and we were able to kill two birds with one vampire hunter."

Rayne scoffed and shook his head. "Like they are going to be able to kill our master. Maybe delay him, but he'll still come for us. There were a few of his minions who saw us make our escape."

I shot a withering glare in Rayne's direction. "Why can't you just let us be happy for one moment? We can worry about them later. I just want to get back to Piper. Where is she, by the way?" I glanced around inside of the car as if she might appear at any moment.

"At the hotel," Marcus said over his shoulder from the front seat next to Darren who was driving.

"Oh." I sank into my seat, disappointed. "That was probably a good idea. I'm assuming the twins are with her."

Antoine inclined his head. "Yes. For the time being. But if Boris does make it out of there alive, then we will need to take him out, permanently."

I cracked my knuckles a feeling of glee came over me. "With pleasure." Being back with my brothers was like a dream, and I would soon be with Piper again. Then we could end this, once and for all.

Chapter 17
Drake

WHILE THE REST OF my brothers went off to save Wynn, my twin and I had the great pleasure of keeping a pissed off Piper from running after them and getting herself and the rest of us killed in the process. To do that, I had a foolproof plan. Well, Allister had a foolproof plan, I was just going to help execute it.

"First up, champagne." I grinned as room service appeared at the door, pushing a cart with a metal ice bowl. Three bottles of what I knew was the finest champagne sat inside the bowl of ice. Three flutes perched on the tray around it.

Piper's lip twitched up, her nose scrunching. "I don't know, Drake. Is this really the time to be drinking?" She turned back to the window and gestured out of it. "We should be out there helping the others bring Wynn back."

"Yes." Allister walked over to her, placing his hands on her shoulder, ushering her farther into the room. "But the others have it. We have to trust them to handle it. And you," he pressed her onto the couch with a bounce, "need to relax. The alcohol will help."

I popped the cork on the champagne and laughed, pouring a heaping amount into a glass. "Here. Drink this." I strolled across the room and shoved it into her hand.

Piper stared skeptically down at the glass. "I'm not much of a drinker. If you think I'm a klutz now, adding alcohol is just going to make me more of a hazard and not just to myself."

"Don't worry, you can't kill us." Allister plopped down beside him, a flute in his hand. When Piper still didn't drink, I sat on the opposite side of her and angled my glass to hers. She reluctantly clinked her glass with mine.

"To Piper!" I cheered and winked. "Who brought us all this far."

With a small smile, Piper took a drink, and then after a moment downed the rest. Gasping, she sagged back into the couch. "I just don't understand why I have to stay here. I mean, wouldn't you guys rather be out there helping with Wynn?"

I reached over and grabbed the bottle of champagne, filling her glass back up. "Of course we would, but keeping you safe is a priority also. Besides..." I leaned in until my face was close to hers. "I'd rather be here with you than out there getting my ass kicked."

Piper giggled and sipped from her glass, finally loosening up a little bit.

"Alright!" Allister jumped to his feet. "We have drinks. Now, it's time for a game." He lifted a box off the table and held it up. "Have you played this before?"

She arched a brow. "Twister? Really? You guys really do want me to fall on my ass tonight, huh?"

"Come on, Piper." I bumped my shoulder with hers. "Live a little. When can you let loose like this back home? Unless you'd rather be back there cleaning the drapes and washing our clothes." I wagged my eyebrows at her. "Washing Allister's jockey shorts can't be easy."

"Hey!" Allister kicked me in the shin. "Yours are way worse than mine."

Piper snorted. "Actually, I would have to give that award to Marcus."

"Really?" I tipped the rest of my champagne and then poured myself another, needing large quantities to even feel a buzz. "Allister, why don't you set up the game and Piper here can give us all the dirt on our brothers."

Drinking deeply from her glass as if she were finally giving in, Piper swallowed and then confessed, "Marcus might be the more mysterious and quieter of the six of you, but he doesn't seem to know what a hamper is. Seriously—" She hiccupped and held her glass out to me for more. "Every single day, I'm spending more time picking up his dirty clothes than anything else. And by the way, why have bedrooms or even beds if you don't even sleep in there? What's up with that?" I watched her with a growing smile as she drank half her glass before she kept going. "And the basement, don't even get me started on the basement. I clean that whole mansion by myself every day and am privy to all of your secrets, but I can't clean your daytime resting place? Such a double standard."

"For real," I agreed, turning my seat so one arm was over the back of the couch and I could watch her. "Are you ready, bro?"

Allister looked up from the ground where he had spread out the plastic mat covered in colored dots. "Yep. Who wants to go first?"

"I will!" Piper held one hand up, her other
holding her glass as she stood, or at least
tried to. She giggled and fell back. I lifted a
hand, giving her ass a boost.

"You weren't kidding," I commented with
a chuckle, watching as she got to her feet
and wobbled over to the mat. Allister smiled
up at her as he handed her the spinner.
Flipping her finger against the plastic piece,
she swayed while waiting for it to stop. When
it did, she stood up quickly, lifting a hand in
the air. "Right foot, red."

Piper spun around to look at the board,
and then with an exaggerated movement,
placed her right food on the red dot. Spinning
around, a bright smile on her lips she
pointed a finger at me. "Your turn!"

Half an hour later, we were all tangled up
on the mat. Piper was stretched over Allister,
who had done a backbend to get to the dot
he was on, and I had a glorious view down
Piper's shirt.

"You know," Piper said, straining to stay
up. "You guys are really nice to stay here and
try to keep my mind off of everything. I don't
know what I'd have done if I'd been stuck
here with Darren."

I snorted and muttered, "Probably be
naked and coming."

"Hey! I heard that." Piper reached out and smacked me with one of her feet, making her toddle and then fall. She knocked into Allister's arm, shoving her butt right into my face—not that I was complaining, but that caused me to lose my balance—and we all went tumbling into a pile of arms and limbs.

Laughing on the ground, we didn't try to get up right away. Piper laid on Allister's chest, her lower half over my hips, smelling absolutely divine and perhaps a little bit aroused by the situation. Unable to help myself, I tested how she would react by sliding my hand up the top of her thigh, my fingers teasing the inner crease. Though Piper never made a sound, her arousal flared, and I inhaled deeply, feeling myself grow hard at just the smell of her.

Glancing up at her, I watched Piper's expression as she lifted her hand to stroke Allister's chest, her face the model of pure contentment. I shifted my gaze to my brother's, wagging my brows suggestively. To Piper, I asked, "Want to play again?"

Piper lifted her hands and sat up. "No, no. Once is enough. I have enough bruises as it is."

"We could play something else," Allister suggested, lifting up to a sitting position as well.

"Sure," Piper agreed, pushing to her feet. "What do you have in mind?" I shot a look over at the deck of cards sitting on the table where Allister had placed them earlier just in case. "We could play poker."

Piper scrunched her nose up. "I'm not that good at it."

"Strip poker it is!" I announced, jumping to my feet and grabbing the cards as Piper giggled.

"Now you're just trying to get me naked." Even as she teased me, her arousal spiked and she subtly pressed her thighs together.

I winked and smirked. "Of course."

Shaking her head as she laughed once more, she grabbed the bottom of her shirt and pulled it over her head, leaving her only in a pale purple lace bra. Allister and I gaped at her. She shrugged, her hands going to her pants. "I'm going to lose anyways, might as well save myself the humiliation of showing you my terrible card playing."

I swallowed thickly, exchanging a look with Allister. I wasn't going to stop her. No way, no how, but my brother...

"Piper." Allister stepped closer to her, reaching out like he meant to stop her from disrobing. "You don't have to do that. We were just teasing. You've had a lot to drink.

We don't want you to feel like we are taking advantage of you."

Tucking her fingers into the waistband of her pants, Piper scowled at us. "Why do men always think that they are taking advantage of a woman? What if I'm taking advantage of you?" She smirked defiantly as she pushed her pants down, revealing a matching lace thong on her lower half.

My mouth grew dry as I stared unabashedly. "Uh, Piper. Far be it from me to stop a gorgeous woman from taking her clothes off, but my brother is right. We don't want you to do something you'll regret."

Piper rolled her eyes, unhooked her bra, and dropped it to the ground. "Look, it's been a long few weeks and honestly, I'm more than fed up. If I'm going to be stuck here while the future of our house and Wynn rests in the others' hands, then I need to feel in control." Stalking toward me where I sat on the floor, she knelt before me, placing a hand on either side of me. "This makes me feel in control. Are you going to take that from me, Drake?"

I shook my head, my mouth agape as I tried and failed not to look at her fabulous breasts.

Setting her hot core against my jean-clad legs, Piper peered coyly over her shoulder at Allister. "What about you?"

Licking his lips, Allister shook his head vehemently. "Nope. No complaints here. You're in charge. Got it."

Piper's hands found the bottom of my shirt and slid beneath it, her hot hands on my cool skin making me shiver. She pulled her lower lip between her teeth, worrying it as if she had to focus to touch me. I kept my hands on the floor, keeping with the she was in charge thing. If that was the way Piper wanted it, then I had no problems making it happen.

She pushed my shirt up and over my stomach, exposing my abs to her greedy gaze. Her nails scratched at my skin and I groaned, curling my fingers into fists so as not to touch her. Her light brown eyes lifted to mine, a small seductive grin on her lips. "Your abs are so amazing. Do you have to work out a lot to keep them, or does being immortal kind of negate all that?"

I shrugged, not at all interested in talking about my workout regiment, neither was my dick, which was shoved up against the inside of my pants. "It doesn't hurt, but it's not necessary." I hissed out a breath when her nails hit my nipple.

Piper smirked and did it again.

"You're killing me here, Piper," I grated through clenched teeth. Allister sat next to us, watching but not coming closer until Piper asked for him to. She giggled and pushed my shirt up all the way, urging me to lift my arms. Not wanting to displease the lady, I pulled the shirt up and over my head.

Her fingers and hands stroked up and down my chest as if she would be completely happy just doing that for the rest of the night. If so, I'd be in for a very cold shower indeed.

"I wonder..." Her hands paused as her gaze drifted over to Allister. "Are you identical in every way?" She cocked a brow, her eyes dipping down to both Allister's and my pants.

Allister smiled slightly, moving closer to us. Without being asked, Allister jerked his shirt over his head, exposing the sigil of our house tattooed on his chest. Piper reached over and traced the lines of the sigil with one hand, the other doing the same to mine.

"Should I get the same tattoo?" she murmured, more to herself than to us. She moved her hands from us to her own chest, tracing the pattern along the top of her left breast. "What do you think?"

My eyes instantly dipped to her breasts, her nipples hardened from the cool room. Cautiously, I lifted my hand and cupped her upper back, my thumb smoothing over her side. "If you want. Darren doesn't have it.

But I could see you getting one." When she didn't protest my touch, I inched my hand around and cupped her left breast. Piper gasped and arched into my caress. "But if you're wanting less attention, that's not the way to get it. I'd never want you to put another shirt on ever."

I tweaked her nipple and then took a chance. Leaning forward, I drew her nipple into my mouth, sucking on it carefully so as not to nick her with my fangs. Piper's fingers curled into my hair, tugging me closer. She must have reached out to Allister too, because he took her other nipple into his mouth as well. Piper's hips jerked against my lap, her arousal filling the room, and I knew she had to be soaking that tiny thong she wore.

Anxious to see her naked, my hand dropped to her hip, pulling her closer to my aching shaft. I dipped my fingers beneath the side of her thong, but before I could rip it off of her, Piper's hand clamped down on mine. I lifted my head from her breast, as did Allister.

Locking her eyes with mine, Piper shook her head. "I'm in charge, remember?"

My lips tugged up at the sides and I released her thong. "Of course. My apologies. You just smell..." I inhaled deeply, growling low in my chest. "So good. I got ahead of myself."

Piper's eyes lit up at my words and she swiveled her hips against the lump in my pants, making me groan once more. "That's because I have two of the hottest guys I've ever met touching me."

Allister grinned and kissed her shoulder. "Likewise."

Piper hummed and placed her hands on one side of each of our faces. "You know, I never daydreamed about twins before I met you two. You make me want to be very, very bad." Her voice lowered into a husky growl.

"Is that so?" I countered, grabbing her bare ass in my hands and giving it a good squeeze. "We can do bad. Can't we, Al?"

Allister gave Piper a wicked grin, unbuttoning his pants slowly as Piper's eyes devoured every inch of him. "Yes, we can do bad. As bad as you want."

Piper's tongue darted out to wet her lips, her breath coming in short pants. "I can see that." While her eyes were on my brother, I rocked her against my front, groaning at the heat coming off of her and aching to be inside her. To my surprise, she let me. I thought she'd have stopped me again, taking full control of it all. However, Piper was entranced by Allister lowering his jeans until his cock jutted out of his pants.

Piper gripped my shoulders tightly, groaning against me and keeping herself from reaching out and touching him. Then her gaze dipped from his lap to mine. "What about you?"

With a lift of one corner of my lips, I reached between us and unsnapped my pants, almost moaning at the feel of her core so close to my hand. Shifting her back a tiny bit, I released my own length from my jeans.

Piper's eyes locked on to me and then darted to Allister's. It wasn't strange to see my brother naked, it wasn't like I hadn't seen him this way before. We've shared women, but not so intimately as it was with Piper.

"They look similar," she noted to herself, and then grasped me in her hand. "But I better check for sure." My hips jutted into her hand, my eyes fluttering closed as Allister let out a grunt. "Ah," Piper murmured, her hand going up and down my cock. "It's uncanny. I for sure thought you would be different, at least here."

"Piper," Allister squeaked out. "If you want to continue, then you better stop now. I don't know how much more I can take."

I snorted. "I obviously have more stamina."

Allister shot me a glare, but Piper released him and me, scooching back into a crouched position. Seeing her like that almost made me shoot my load. *Damn, she was sexy.*

"Strip," Piper commanded me, her eyes eating up every inch of my body as I shed my pants. She sat up, her fingers teasing the sides of her thong. Allister's and my eyes burned into her skin as she pulled the thong one way and then the other, revealing small inches of herself to us at a time. When she was completely bare, her arousal hit the room full force.

"Fuck," I grunted, and Allister answered with his own curse.

Piper chewed on her lower lip once more as she toyed with something she wanted to say. "Is it strange for you?"

"Is what strange?" Allister questioned. I couldn't get two words put together in the face of a naked and ready Piper.

"For me to want you both at the same time." Her cheeks flushed a pretty pink like she was ashamed of her own wants.

I shook my head, finally pulling my gaze away from her center. "No, not at all. We wouldn't have it any other way. Right, Al?"

Allister nodded. A jerking movement that made him look like a bobble head.

"How do we do this then?" Piper shifted on her heels, her gaze moving between us. "I've never...at the same time."

It was our turn to take control. A wolfish grin covered my lips and Allister matched mine with one of his own. Crawling toward her on our hands and knees, we stopped before her, mere inches away from touching her. This wasn't our first threesome virgin, but hopefully Piper would be our last. I couldn't imagine being with anyone else and I was sure my brother felt the same.

Piper couldn't seem to figure out which one of us to go to first, so to save herself some guilt, I reached out to her, cupping a hand behind her neck and pulling her into a kiss. She stilled against me, but then after some prompting, opened her mouth beneath me. I dipped my tongue inside as Allister moved up behind her. I felt his fingers brush against me as he cupped her breasts. Piper moaned into my kiss, arching her back into Allister's hands.

Kissing her a few more moments, I pulled back. "Since this is your first time, we don't have to both be inside you at the same time. We could work our way up to it."

Piper shook her head. "No. I want you both. Right now." She winced and then added on, "Just go slow."

Allister and I exchanged a look over her shoulder. We'd done this before, and Allister was the more gentle of us two and had the most control. Which was important for someone who had never had anal sex, let alone sex with two people at the same time.

I lifted Piper into my arms, sliding Piper over my pulsating cock. The head of it bumped against her entrance, making her gasp and moan, grinding herself greedily against me. "Slowly now, babe. Isn't that what you said?"

Piper threw her head back in aggravation. "Fuck what I said, just get inside me now."

Smirking at her eagerness, I pressed a hot kiss to her lips. "You're the boss." I reached between us and lined us up before pushing her down onto me. We both let out a moan of pleasure. Piper wrapped her legs around my waist, taking over our movements. If I could breathe, my breath would have caught at the rapid rhythm she started. I could barely keep up with her and found myself getting close to the edge before I knew it.

"Whoa, slow down." I grabbed her hips and decreased her pace until the feel of her moving on me was more of an agonizing ache than a full-on throttle.

Piper grunted. "Please, now." She tried to take over once more.

Holding back a laugh at her impatience, I ushered Allister forward. If we were going to do this, we'd have to do it soon, before Piper lost her patience and I didn't have the willpower to stop her.

Allister stroked his hand up her back before sliding it down between them. Piper moaned at the contact, shifting her hips backward as Allister moved his fingers to her backside. She gasped and I felt a prodding from the inside of her, and I knew Allister was getting her ready. The scissoring movement of his fingers pushed against my restraint, and I had to close my eyes to keep myself from just going for it already.

Allister moved in close and Piper groaned as a new pressure pushed against the inside of her. I released her waist to find her clit between us, rubbing it in slow circles to get her to relax as Allister pressed completely into her. With both of us inside her, Piper's heartbeat sped up and her insides squeezed me tight.

Signaling Allister with my head, we started a synchronized rhythm. Piper rocked between us, sliding up and down my length. The added pressure of Allister on the other side of her heightened everything. Piper's arousal and the slapping of flesh only added to my need. I wasn't going to last much longer, and from the way my brother grunted and Piper's cries of pleasure grew, I knew they weren't much further behind.

Just as Piper let out a long, drawn out scream, voices came from the other side of the door. We barely had the chance to come down from our release before the hotel room door was thrown open. Piper squeaked and twisted around, pressed between Allister and myself, our bodies covering most of her from the prying eyes of all four of my brothers—Wynn included.

Wynn grinned down at the scene before him. "Looks like I missed out on all the fun."

Chapter 18
Rayne

THE MOMENT PIPER SAW Wynn, she shoved herself from between the twins and ran for him, naked and all. Darren and Marcus averted their gazes, but I simply shook my head and pushed into the room. I needed a drink.

Antoine followed close behind me while Piper flung herself into Wynn's arms. The vampire chuckled and held her close. "While I am happy to see you too, love, why don't we get you some clothes, eh?"

Piper's eyes widened and shot down to her body before she let out an ear-piercing shriek. She pressed herself closer to Wynn, trying to hide her nude form from the rest of us. Even though all but two of us had seen her naked before.

Fuck. Fuck. Fuck. I'm naked in a room full of vamps.

I lifted my eyes to the ceiling and sighed.

Correction. I'm naked in a room full of vamps after I just had sex with two of them at the same time! Oh, my God. I'm going to hell, aren't I?"

This thought caused me to chuckle. Piper's horrified gaze zeroed in on me, her lips pursed as she narrowed her eyes. "Will you get out of my head? I'm already traumatized enough."

I shrugged, picking up the glass of blood I'd taken from the fridge. "I don't know why. It's not like we haven't all seen you naked before. Well, except for Marcus." My brows furrowed as I glanced over at Darren. "Have you seen her naked or was it a clothes on kind of situation?"

Piper groaned in mortification the longer I went on.

Wynn patted her on the shoulder and then held his hand out to the twins, who were still sitting on the ground, not really caring at all about their nudity. "Give me your shirt."

Drake pulled his shirt from the pile of discarded clothes and handed it over.

"Arms up, lovely."

Piper lifted her arms, allowing Wynn to drop the shirt over her head. Drake's shirt came down to just under her ass, hiding all that delicious skin from view. I understood her discomfort, but once everyone saw you in the nude it was kind of pointless to cover it all up—we were all thinking about it anyway. Not to mention the room stunk of sex and Piper's arousal.

As if reading my thoughts, Marcus walked quickly across the room and opened several windows. All of the vampires sagged in relief.

Should I go get cleaned up? I kind of want to know what happened. I don't want to miss it just to take a shower. Plus, Piper's scent on my dick is getting me hard again.

I scrunched my face up in disgust at Drake's thoughts. "Dude, go take a shower already. We'll wait until you get back."

Drake didn't chastise me for reading his thoughts for once. He nudged his brother in the arm and they both got up and went into one of the bedrooms. A few moments later, the shower turned on, and low voices that I couldn't make out from this distance whispered back and forth.

Piper finally released Wynn long enough to go into the bedroom herself. Her thoughts raced too fast for me to hear and I mentally blocked her out. I didn't need her pissed off at me when we were in such a dire situation.

With a glass of the champagne the twins had ordered, I leaned against the kitchenette counter. "So, this is awkward."

Wynn snorted a laugh as he lounged in one of the armchairs.

Antoine sat on the couch with a pensive expression on his face, not reacting to my comment.

Darren passed out glasses of blood to Wynn, Marcus, and Antoine before standing off to the side of the couch. That man didn't know when to relax.

I skimmed the others' minds, looking for some kind of clue that they were feeling put out by the fact that Piper had slept with the twins. Thankfully, none of them seemed to care—except Marcus, he wasn't thinking about anything.

It didn't bother me. Per se. It did make me feel a bit worried. While our family had shared a woman before, it was never in this aspect. There were feelings involved. Feelings that might get hurt if we weren't all up front with how we felt.

Antoine's gaze lifted to mine. "I know what you're thinking, Rayne." When I balked in horror, he added, "It's written all over your face. Unfortunately, now is not the time." His pale eyes shifted to the closed bedroom door. "I'm fine with it all and if I'm not mistaken, Wynn and the twins are too." Wynn nodded in agreement, sipping from his glass. "Do not cause yourself more worry than necessary. Once this is all over, we will discuss it."

Understanding his words but not liking them, I jerked a nod and then walked over to Piper's bedroom. The twins' door opened before I could knock on hers. They gave me a curious glance before moving into the living area. I knocked softly on Piper's door.

"Yes?"

"Are you decent? We are about to start." There was some shuffling and then Piper let out a hiss.

"Fuck."

My lips quirked up at the sides. She'd hit something again. The klutz.

"Piper?" I prodded, listening to make sure she wasn't seriously injured.

The door flung open and Piper's out of breath, red face peered back at me. "Yeah. I'm ready. Had a little mishap."

I arched a brow. "So I heard." Her blonde hair clung to the sides of her face from the quick shower she had taken, and she'd changed out of Drake's shirt, pulling on a pair of black yoga pants and a baggy top. I didn't know if it was because she was uncomfortable wearing his shirt or if she knew that having Drake's scent all over her would drive the rest of us crazy.

Either way, I was thankful.

"Let's go." Piper pushed past me and into the sitting room.

I followed after her. Piper hesitated, her mind swirling over where to sit. After a moment, she settled on the arm of Wynn's chair, apparently unable to be far from him for long.

"So, what's the plan?" Piper asked. "Do we go home now?" I could hear the hopefulness in her voice.

I hated to burst her bubble, so I left that to Antoine as I sat by the window, staring down into the street. It was quiet. No one would have known we'd been battling hunters a few miles away.

Antoine made a disgruntled sound in his throat. "Unfortunately, that is not an option yet. We still have to take care of Boris."

I watched Piper out of the corner of my eye. Her face scrunched up in irritation. "What's there to take care of? Didn't the hunters do their job? We got Wynn back, why can't we just leave him to his fate?"

Wynn placed a hand on Piper's leg, smoothing it up and down in a soothing manner. "It's not that simple, pet."

"Boris is far from dead," Marcus, to my surprise, spoke up.

Piper groaned and slapped her hand down on her leg. "Then what are the hunters good for? They can't kill one lousy vampire?"

"You forget." Antoine leveled a stare at her. "Boris is more than just any vampire. He's a master vampire. Perhaps even stronger than me or all of us put together. It was a fool's hope that the hunters would be able to take him out."

"Okay. So then we just take off and leave him to his fancy parties." Piper waved a hand in front of her.

Drake snorted a laugh. "If you think Boris will leave us alone after this, you are delusional."

"Exactly," Allister added, looking to his brother. "Not only did we steal Wynn back, but we sicced the hunters on him. A big no-no in the vampire community. We basically committed treason." Allister shrugged a shoulder. "Against him anyway. Not that I give a shit what he thinks, but he will retaliate if we don't take him out first."

Piper chewed on her lower lip, worry etched on her face. "Then what do we do?"

Antoine uncrossed his legs and recrossed them. "We go in now while he is disoriented and hopefully injured from the battle."

Piper narrowed her eyes on him. "You're going to make me stay behind again, aren't you?"

The tension in the room thickened. There was no doubt in any of our minds that Piper would be a liability if not a distraction. We couldn't take out Boris and whoever else might be left and worry about keeping her safe. It would be best for everyone if she stayed behind.

Antoine, however, didn't immediately tell her no. "Tell me, Piper, if you come face to face with Boris on your own, what would you do?"

Piper shifted uncomfortably in her spot by Wynn. I could tell she wanted to say something badass, but she straightened and stared Antoine down. "I'd run in the opposite direction."

We could smell the lie before she even finished saying it.

Antoine's lips quirked up bitterly. "No. You're not coming." Piper opened her mouth to argue, but Antoine didn't let her cut into him this time. "I cannot trust you to do as you're told, and unless you wish to convert into a vampire right this moment, giving you a tiny bit of extra protection to your human form, you will stay behind even if I have to knock you out again."

Piper opened and shut her mouth like a fish, then clamped it shut. She didn't want to be a vampire. It was clear on her face. At least not this second. Even if she wanted to come with us, it wasn't something she was willing to do.

Finally. A line she wouldn't cross.

With a huff, Piper stood and walked out of the room. For once not slamming the door behind her.

"You shouldn't have done that," Wynn pointed out, worry tugging his lips down into a frown. "Now she will always be connecting changing into one of us with this moment."

Antoine lifted a shoulder nonchalantly. "It had to be done. I won't lose her again or any of us because of it."

"Still..." Wynn stroked his fingers through his dark hair. "There is going to be backlash with her even if we all get out of this alive."

"Do you plan on dying today, Wynn?" Drake antagonized him with a quirk of his brow.

Wynn gave him a rakish grin. "Not today. Not for a long while." A wistful look came over him, his gaze shifting to where Piper had gone, lingering there for a while. He wanted to go to her. It was written all over his face, I didn't need to read his mind to know.

"Darren," Antoine continued, waving his human servant forward, "will you make sure Piper stays here? Do what you need to in order to keep her safe."

"Of course, master." He placed a hand on his chest and bowed slightly.

Antoine's brows furrowed. "And if something goes wrong, take Piper and go to Seabrick. Wait for orders there."

"As you wish." Darren bowed once more before walking into the kitchen. They didn't embrace or say goodbye like a normal couple would have. Then again, their relationship had never been normal.

I trust him.

Darren's thoughts penetrated my mind and made me long for that kind of relationship with Piper. We were on our way, but too much had happened to really have the time to build our relationship the way Antoine and Darren had. Something I planned to remedy once this was all over.

"Alright." I stood and clapped my hands together. "Let's get this over with. I need a nap and some snuggle time."

The twins and Wynn chuckled at me, but Antoine simply smiled. Yeah, we were all gonna need some snuggle time after this.

Chapter 19
Antoine

THE MANOR BORIS AND his company had housed themselves in was the same one we used to live in back in the day. With bright yellow siding and stone columns all around it, it hadn't changed except for the foliage that had overgrown in the yard. Large trees hid part of the house, and bushes that stood up to my shoulders surrounded the outside of the structure. They were almost making this too easy.

"Ugh." Rayne stared at the manor. "What a dump. Are you sure this is where he's at?"

"Yep." Drake clamped a hand on Rayne's shoulder. "You were lucky not to have ever stayed here. It's cramped, the hallways are too narrow, and the plumbing sucks. Or at least it did."

"Whatever you remember about this place, put it out of your head. A lot in Sofia has changed over the last few decades," I reminded them, shifting in our hiding spot behind some of the bushes. "We don't know what we are going to go up against in there. How many are left. If they are injured."

"If we have any luck at all, Boris will be laid up and needing to feed," Allister noted with hope filling his voice. "I'd like to get this over and done with."

"As would I," I murmured.

A crunch of leaves alerted us to a new presence. We all spun around to see Wynn and Marcus coming back from scouting the house.

"Be a little louder why don't you?" Rayne scoffed, glaring at Wynn's feet.

Giving Rayne a lazy grin, Wynn gestured to the house. "It's practically deserted. There are a few lights on around back, and from what we could see, only Theresa, Boris, and a few guards made it out."

"How'd they look?" Drake anxiously asked, his brows raised. "Please tell me they are dying as we speak."

Shaking his head, Wynn sighed. "Unfortunately, no. Theresa seemed to have sustained some injuries, but Boris looked fine."

"Damn," Allister cursed, and I seconded the notion.

"Very well." I turned to the group and peered through the darkness at their faces. "We will go in as two teams. Allister, Drake." The twins stood at attention at my words. "You take out the remaining guards. Rayne—" The redhead shifted uncomfortably, crossing and uncrossing his arms in an anxious gesture. "You keep back and listen for any thoughts you might pick up, alerting us to any other people in the house."

"What should I do?" Wynn nonchalantly questioned, though his shoulders were tense with the need to get moving.

"Since Theresa still holds a candle for you, can you lure her away? Take her out if you wish, but we need Boris alone." Wynn nodded at my instructions. I turned my gaze to Marcus last. "You and I will confront Boris. When the others have taken out their targets, they will join us. I have a feeling we are going to need all of us to take him down."

"Understood." Marcus pushed his shoulders back, his expression dark and ready for a fight.

I inclined my head to each of my brothers in turn. "Let us get this over with. We will reconvene two blocks north if something goes astray." I began to turn back toward the house, but Wynn spoke up.

"What if the hunters make another appearance? There's no way Boris took them all out. They're like roaches. The more of them you kill, the more of them show up."

My lips curled up in a wicked grin. "Then we kill them all."

We split apart, the twins going around one side while Wynn walked straight down the walkway to the front door. I supposed he was going for the direct approach. Whatever got Theresa away from Boris worked for me. Marcus and I hung back as we waited for them to get into position. We didn't want to alert Boris to our presence until the last possible second.

"Why don't you use one of your pets to check the house?" Marcus asked me a few minutes later.

I frowned at his suggestion. "And let Boris know we are coming? Not likely. They might do as I ask, but keeping them quiet is near impossible."

The crows on our house sigil weren't just there for decoration. It signified who ran the house. Me. The crow was my creature, and while I didn't like to use my powers on them often, they did come in handy in situations such as these. If it had been any other enemy than Boris, I wouldn't have hesitated. Unfortunately, my creator knew every aspect of my powers, including my ability to control crows. It would be a dead giveaway that we were here, and I wasn't going to let him get away that easily.

When there was no immediate alerting of the guards after Wynn entered the manor, Marcus and I moved closer. Taking it slow, we inched across the lawn and up onto the stone porch. I pressed my ear to the wall, thankful for the lack of insulation in the house. They hadn't updated as much as I would have thought.

"Wynn, why, we thought we lost you back there." Boris's tone held both warning and suspicion in its depths. "I am glad to see you are unharmed and have returned to your rightful home."

There was a pause, and then Wynn replied, "I made a deal. I am nothing if not an honorable vampire."

"As that seems," Boris drawled, and then went into a fit of coughs.

"Master," Theresa cried out, her footsteps racing across the wooden floors. "You must lie down. I will get a donor for you right away."

"I'm fine, Theresa. It's only a scratch. I will heal on my own." The annoyance in Boris's voice was clear as day. The fact that he hadn't hit her for her concern was telling about how injured he actually was. Boris didn't want anyone to know he had been hurt during the fight. Especially not Wynn, who he already suspected of treachery.

"Is there anything I can do for you, master?" Wynn inquired, pushing the faithful servant routine.

There was a pause and then Boris said, "You can take Theresa upstairs so she will stop flittering around me like a mother hen. I am twelve hundred years old. I do not need to be coddled."

"Of course, master." There was a hint of a smile in Wynn's voice and then footsteps started toward us.

Backing away from the door, I held a hand up to Marcus to be quiet. When Wynn and Theresa's footsteps pounded up the stairs, I waved a hand for Marcus to come. I wasn't sure where the others were on their missions, but I couldn't let this chance get away from me.

Easing the front door open, I slipped inside with Marcus close behind me. My gaze darted up the stairs where Wynn had disappeared. No one appeared at the top of the landing, which was a relief. I glanced down the narrow hallway that hadn't changed any since the last time I'd lived here. It seemed that Boris didn't care too much about updating this property like his others.

Drake and Allister peeked out from the kitchen, giving me a nod. They had taken out the guards lingering back there. I didn't sense anyone near us, and it sounded like Boris was now alone in the parlor.

I took one step toward the doorway, but stopped as Boris called out, "Come in already. Hiding in the shadows is not your style, Antoine."

Exchanging a look with Marcus, we stepped into the parlor. Boris laid on the couch, his hand clutching his side. Blood tinged the air.

"You're injured," I stated, a feeling of triumph coming over me. This would be easier than I thought.

Boris lifted his hand from his side where blood came away as he coughed a laugh. "Ah, yes. Damn hunters. Their arrows are poisonous to us, as you well know. It slows our healing abilities." His red tinged eyes narrowed on me. "It was cowardly of you to send the hunters to do your dirty work."

I lifted my hands and smiled sardonically. "I learn from the best."

Boris smiled back a bit too brightly. "As do I."

Not even a second later, the windows around us shattered. Commands were shouted and hunters poured in through the windows. Marcus pulled his knives out of his boots and prepared to fight. My mind raced with the different outcomes of this battle. While the fact that Boris was as good as dead was a plus, the likelihood of us getting out of here alive, let alone without being seen, was impossible.

"Duck!" Marcus shouted right as a bolt came at my head.

I dropped down just in time, throwing my leg out and knocking a nearby hunter's legs out from under him. The twins came barreling into the room a moment later. We fought around Boris as he laughed and coughed, the scent of blood growing thick in the air. He wouldn't last much longer, even if a hunter killed him now.

As I dodged another bolt, I spun around and took in the fight. Rayne had come in at some point, fighting off his own hunter. Wynn had yet to join the battle, which meant he was still busy with Theresa. I hoped he stayed out of view, because the rest of us were well and truly screwed.

"There are too many of them!" Drake yelled, swinging a fist into the face of one hunter and then kicking another. The twins stood back to back as they fought off the hunters, each of them taking out one and then another. But they kept coming. This was pointless. We had to get out of here.

"Durands," I called out, backing toward the door. "To me."

Rayne ducked under the arm of a hunter, jabbing him in the stomach before racing to my side. The twins head-butted the hunter in front of them almost as if their minds were in sync. They, too, rushed to my side as we backed out of the room. Marcus was the only one who was lagging behind, unable to get the gaggle of hunters off of him long enough to get out of there.

"Let's go!" Rayne swiped a hand at his bleeding nose. "Marcus, stop playing around."

Marcus took the back of two hunters' shirts and slammed them into each other. With them unconscious, he threw them at the horde of hunters, knocking them back far enough for him to get away.

I stopped at the bottom of the stairs and called up, "Wynn, get out of there!"

Not waiting for him to answer, my brothers and I ran out of the house, the hunters right on our heels. We didn't stop moving until we got two blocks away, as was planned, ducking into a nearby building.

"What about Wynn?" Rayne grabbed the front of my shirt, anger and panic in his voice. "We can't just leave him. Not again. Piper will never forgive us." He slammed his fist against my chest, his eyes closed tightly.

"She won't be happy with us regardless." I took him by the wrists, removing them from my shirt. "We can't go back there. Not with the hunters on our trail. We can't stay here long either. If Wynn is not back in—"

"What? You were going to leave without me?"

"Wynn!" Rayne's eyes shot open and he lunged for our other brother, bringing him into a tight hug. "I thought we'd lost you...again."

Wynn brushed his thumb against the side of his lip with a smirk. "Sorry, I got caught up."

"I'm glad to see you were able to get out okay. Did any of the hunters see you?" I glanced over him, searching for any other sign of a wound.

Wynn grimaced. "Unfortunately, yes. Several tried to take me out while I was attempting to sneak out of the upstairs window."

"That's unfortunate." I sighed and ran a hand over my face. This was not going according to the plan. Killing Boris, yes. Having him turn my own plan against me? I never saw it coming. It wouldn't happen again.

"What about Theresa and Boris?" Drake asked, coming in close, his eyes darting around for any signs of the hunters. "Did you see what happened?"

"Theresa is taken care of." Wynn gave a wicked snarl. "As for Boris, he was being cut to pieces in the parlor from what I heard."

"So, you never saw him actually die?" Allister sighed with annoyance. "What are we going to do?"

"We have to leave. Now. Get as far away from here as possible."

"And what about Darren and Piper?" Rayne questioned, his lips turned down into a frown. "Are we just supposed to leave them without an explanation?"

I pulled my phone out. "I'll message Darren. He has his instructions. But we can't risk going back. We have to move now."

"Piper is going to kill us," Rayne said then groaned, placing his face in his hands. I couldn't disagree.

Chapter 20
Piper

THREE MONTHS. IT HAD been three months since the guys had gone into hiding. Or whatever it was they were doing. Leading the hunters on a wild goose chase for all I knew. Not like they kept up with communication.

I tried to call Antoine for the fifth time that day and it went straight to voicemail. Groaning in frustration, I tossed my phone back into my purse and kept walking down the street of the little town we'd taken up residence in. The town called Seabrick sat on the coast of Georgia, where we'd flown back to the moment we could. There was no way we were going to stay in Sofia. Too many vampires. Plus, the lingering hunters could spot us at any moment. We didn't want to take the chance.

Even though we weren't working for the Durands anymore, Darren and I were still getting a paycheck. We noticed it the second week we were here, and it only made me more pissed off and anxious to find them. In a form of silent protest, I refused to use any of the money they had given me. Instead, I went into Seabrick on the fifteenth day we were here and found a job as a receptionist. It wasn't an exciting job, not by a long shot, but it paid the bills and I didn't have to worry about washing blood off the carpet or cleaning anyone's toilet. Though, my boss was an outrageous flirt who wouldn't give up.

I didn't know how to tell him I was actually dating five guys at once. If you could call it dating. None of them had actually taken me on a date. We mostly just had sex and flirted around the house. Something I was determined to fix when they came back. If they came back.

Holding my heels in my hands, I walked the final few steps to the hotel suite Darren and I shared.

Although we hadn't had sex again, Darren and I had become quite close in our isolation. They hadn't just abandoned me. They had abandoned both of us. Darren seemed to be taking it a lot better than I was. Then again, Darren bottled a lot of things up inside. Sometimes I wished I had Rayne's powers to mind read.

Speaking of Darren, he spent most of his days in the hotel room making calls and doing something on the computer. He once told me he was making arrangements, but for what I didn't know. It wasn't like we had a house to keep up with anymore.

When I walked through the hotel room door, Darren was nowhere to be found, but someone else was. I threw my purse and shoes down in a nearby chair and darted for the large vampire. "Marcus!" I hugged him tightly, though he stiffened at my embrace. I didn't care, I was just happy to see one of them after all this time.

Marcus grunted and softly pushed me away.

I dropped my arms and stepped back a foot. "What are you doing here? Not that I'm complaining, but I haven't heard from you guys in months and then out of nowhere you show up!" I couldn't suppress my excitement and found myself throwing my arms around him again. "Oh, I'm just so happy to see you."

"Piper." Darren's voice made me pull away to glance past Marcus.

Darren came out of the bathroom wearing his usual butler attire. Don't ask me, I had long since grown tired of telling him he didn't need to wear it anymore. He swore it was like a second skin to him and taking it off would be like giving up. I didn't disagree, but a part of me still wanted to see Darren in something other than a suit. If his slacks did anything for his butt now, I couldn't wait to see him in some jeans.

Jerking my thoughts away from Darren's ass, I glanced down at the bloody towel in his hands. "What's going on?" When Darren didn't answer, I turned my attention back to Marcus. "Are you hurt?" I searched him for some kind of injury but found none. "What's with the blood?"

Darren tossed the towel onto the nearby counter, something I never saw him do before. He was all about keeping things neat and orderly. In fact, the first thing he did when we got here was go buy a laundry basket and cleaning supplies. Like he didn't trust the hotel staff to take care of it.

"No, I'm not hurt," Marcus answered in his low voice. "I was a bit rough."

My brows furrowed in confusion as my mind wrapped around what Marcus had said. Then, like a lightbulb went off, my eyes widened and my mouth dropped open into an O-shape. "Gotcha. But why did you need to feed on Darren? Couldn't you have taken someone else on the way here?"

Marcus shook his head but didn't elaborate.

Darren stepped up beside us and explained, "The hunters are watching everywhere for them. Any sign of one of them taking blood from someone will alert them to their presence. It is safer for him to take blood from me."

I nodded dumbly, then asked, "What about the others? How are they feeding then?"

Marcus didn't answer, allowing Darren to take point. "They're in one of our safe houses up north. I won't say where because it isn't secure. We never know who could be listening in. All you need to know is that they are safe for now and have plenty of blood stored up there to get them where they need to go next."

"Which is where?"

"I don't know yet," Darren supplied with a helpless shrug.

I sighed and sat down on the bed with an ungraceful thump. I was tired of getting secondhand information. I wanted to hear it from the horse's mouth. Or rather the vampire's mouth. Why hadn't they called? If they were at a safe house, why couldn't they contact us? Why send Marcus?

Shooting a look to the large vampire, I asked what I was thinking.

"To protect you," Marcus grunted.

Bracing my hands on the bed, I glanced around the room. "Protect us from what? Boredom?"

Shaking his head, Marcus didn't answer, letting Darren once more be the bearer of bad news. "Someone leaked information to the hunters that we were here. They might come for us, trying to lure the others out."

My heart rate ratcheted in my chest at the thought of the others getting hurt because of me. I'd had enough of them sacrificing for me. I wasn't about to let it happen again. If the hunters were coming for us, then we couldn't stay here. We would have to move around like the guys were. Except I had a feeling it wouldn't be that simple. We couldn't just meet up with them and let them protect us. No, we'd be a distraction they didn't need. No matter how much I wanted to be with them right now, I couldn't. I'd have to settle for my dreams to get me through this time—even though they were of my own creation and not a connection to any of my guys.